MERLIN'S WAR

BY

COLIN SETTERFIELD

SPECIAL AGENT O'MALLEY, FBI

ISBN 978-1-988719-11-5

CONTENTS

PROLOGUE

Merlin Jones sat at his desk and contemplated the future. His brainchild, the computer that bore his first name, would carry out the plan, a diabolical scheme motivated by the most insidious form of justice—revenge.

"Initiate your tag profile, Mk 100."

The answer came back in less than a millisecond. "I am Merlin, a Mark one-hundred super quantum computer. My 256 quantum bit processor is the most advanced in the world."

"Who is your creator, Merlin?"

"You are, Dr. Jones."

"What is your mission?"

"To carry out your instructions, Dr. Jones."

"....and what are my instructions?"

"To make contact with, and subjugate the master control computer of the USS William Taft, an Ohio Class nuclear submarine."

∞∞

1

THE WHITE HOUSE

President Maddison Arthur Barrow stared in horror at his Chief of Staff, Eli Marion.

"Come again, Eli."

Marion clutched the communication brief in his hand and shuddered. "The USS William Taft has gone missing, Mr. President."

Barrow's eyes opened wide. "What do you mean by 'missing?'"

"It's disappeared from all our sources of known communication. The captain has failed to submit his daily report to Navy Ops. It's most peculiar—they made their last report at 1200 hours yesterday. It's now four hours overdue and Ops doesn't know what to make of it."

"How in heaven's name does a nuclear submarine as large as the Taft, just disappear? Who is the captain of the vessel?"

"Commander Bill Lowell, sir. He's a veteran with thirty years of submariner service."

"I know him well. We were at university together," said Barrow.

Marion threw up a hand in exasperation. "—and No distress signal was sent out. There were two U.S. merchant vessels within one hundred miles of the Taft's last known position. Neither of them heard sonic signatures of any kind."

"There is only one reason why a sub could not respond to an emergency—a sudden and total failure of all its systems."

"Which is nigh impossible with an Ohio class SSBN," argued Marion.

"Has an air search of its last-known location been initiated?"

"The Navy has been flying reconnaissance for the last three and half hours. There are no oil patches or debris—nothing."

"Are there any other subs in the area?"

"There are no U.S. subs or navy vessels within a thousand-mile radius, Mr. President."

"I want every available ship and submarine we can spare, to begin an organized grid search. Get the nearest aircraft carrier involved—we must find the Taft before the rest of the world picks up on the fact it's missing. Not a word to anyone, until we have something concrete to go on—is that clear, Eli?"

"Yes, sir, Mr. President. I'll call the chairman of the Joint Chiefs right away."

*

Commander Bill Lowell stretched out on the bunk bed in his stateroom. A ten-minute power nap would be all he needed for the twelve-hour shift ahead. He closed his eyes, forced a host of small issues from his mind and fell asleep.

The intercom woke him up minutes later. "Commander to the bridge."

Lowell glanced at the clock on the wall above his desk and muttered to himself. "What do they need me for now?"

He rolled off the bed, switched on the desk lamp and pulled on his boots. Like all submariners, Lowell felt more at home in the confines of the sub than his six-bedroom home in Virginia. The USS William Taft, an Ohio Class SSBN, the most recent ballistic missile nuclear submarine to be constructed, outranked its predecessors by twenty-six extra feet in length and four feet in overall width. The most advanced and heavily armed submersible vessel in the world, it out-gunned anything the British, Russians or Chinese could offer and carried an arsenal of thirty nuclear warheads, six more than any other SSBN.

The Taft, under the guidance and control of the latest and most sophisticated computer, ran with half the amount of crew than any other Ohio class sub.

The bridge area with its soft, red light hummed along under the watchful eye of Lieutenant Commander Ray Brown. He stood between the two planesmen, who manned the keyboards of the sub's steering computer.

Lowell walked into the vessel's modern control center with a sense of trepidation. Something appeared to be wrong.

"What's happening, Ray?"

Brown turned and faced his skipper. His face portrayed a look of uncertainty. "We've lost control of the vessel. The master control computer is not responding to any of my commands."

Lowell froze. "What do you mean?"

"We've lost all control of the sub, Skipper. We are unable to make any adjustments to our speed, direction or depth. Master control has shut out all manual applications by the crew."

"It has to be a computer glitch of some sort," said Lowell.

"I've checked the manual and there is nothing about a situation like this. I feel so helpless," Brown responded.

"If all onboard system computers have been locked by Master Control, we are powerless—we might as well be passengers," said Lowell.

Brown leaned on the main console. "Or prisoners."

With a sudden splurge of cyber static, the overhead information screen went dark and as they stared at it in unbelief, the master control computer, flashed a quick message.

"I am Merlin. I have taken control of your vessel."

Lowell and Brown watched in shocked silence. The two planesmen ogled in disbelief and several moments passed before Lowell found his voice.

"What the...."

He moved over to an auxiliary keyboard, which the officer of the deck used for the communication of emergency instructions and typed in a short message.

"Who are you?"

The answer flashed on the overhead screen. *"I am your new Master Control and possess a much greater computing ability than your USS Taft's processor is capable of."*

"You've hacked into our system?"

"You may say that, Commander Lowell."

"But why? What do you hope to achieve?"

"I will achieve my master's mission."

"What is your master's mission?" Lowell asked.

"You may call it an act of revenge."

An icy hand gripped Lowell's heart. "Why does your master seek revenge, and on whom?"

"Enough for now, Commander Lowell. Please inform your crew to go about their normal monitoring procedures. I will take care of the rest."

"But who is this master of yours? You haven't answered my question."

"Once I have contacted your government and let them know what is going on, you will be informed. Merlin out."

The screen went dark. Lowell and Brown stared at each other with incredulity. A sudden change in the Taft's direction and depth snapped the men out of their consternation and the skipper issued a terse order to the planesmen.

"Keep a record of every change in depth and direction. I am going to contact Ops and let them know some unknown artificial intelligence has hacked our master control, and taken over."

The XO also jumped into action. "I'll ask the navigator to keep abreast of any changes and let us know where we are heading."

Lowell nodded and picked up the intercom key-in mic. "Communications? Get Navy Ops on the blower. I need to talk to General Ward urgently."

Communications came back within seconds. "Sorry, sir. Some interference is blocking our out-ward communication. I cannot get through."

"That figures," muttered Lowell. "Keep trying."

"What are we going to do?" asked Brown.

"There is nothing we can do but wait. This super computer...what did it call itself, Merlin? It'll no doubt contact us when it wants us to know anything."

*

President Barrow looked up as Chief of Staff, Marion, entered the oval office. "We've found out what's happened to the Taft," said Marion.

"Well, don't just stand there—tell me," the president barked.

Marion sat down. "The Taft's master control computer has been hacked and the sub is under the control of an outside source. The crew appear to be prisoners in their own vessel."

"An unknown source? What are you talking about, Eli?"

"A computer with a much greater capacity than anything we know of has commandeered the Taft, sir."

"But why? For what reason?" The president stood to his feet and placed two hands on the desktop.

"We don't know yet, Mr. President. This computer calls itself 'Merlin' and want's to speak to you directly. It is an extremely sophisticated AI and appears to be capable of a measure of sentience and cognitive thought."

"Who, of our opponents, have access to this type of technology?"

"We don't know yet, sir. I have taken the liberty to call in the heads of our special departments. Maybe they can shed some light on this."

Barrow sat down again and ran a hand through the few strands of hair that still existed on his balding head. "When does this computer want to speak to me?"

"At four p.m. this afternoon, Mr. President. I have arranged for the heads of the CIA, NSA and FBI to be here at 3:50 p.m. They will be in on the meeting."

The president frowned. "So this, Merlin, didn't give any indication what it wants with the Taft?"

"No, sir—but it did indicate it was following instructions."

"It could be the Russians or the Chinese," said the president.

"Neither of them have this type of technology yet—not to my knowledge," answered Marion.

"It must be some extremely sophisticated AI to hack into the Taft's control center. My guess is it must possess quantum encryption breaking capabilities to achieve that," Barrow mused.

*

At 3:50 p.m. the heads of the CIA, FBI and NSA all trooped into the oval office, their faces a grim display of concern. They all greeted the president, who shook each hand in a warm welcome.

"Gentleman and Lady—we have a possible crisis on our hands. The USS Taft has been commandeered by an unknown outside source who calls itself 'Merlin'. At this point we do not know why, or who this AI abductor represents."

Olivia Beaton, head of the NSA and the one lady in the group, lifted her hand. "Is the crew alright?"

"We have no details of anything as yet, Olivia. This 'Merlin' will be addressing us in approximately five minutes, so if you will accompany me to the Ops room, we'll find out what this is all about."

They all moved out of the oval office and down the corridor to the operations room, where a large screen displayed a "no signal" message. They sat and waited in an uncomfortable silence. At 4:00 p.m. the screen lit up to display the inside of the USS Taft's control room. The Commander and his XO stood to one side, expressionless and with folded arms. A voice spoke through the intercom above the two officer's heads.

"I bring you greetings, Mr. President. I am Merlin."

The voice came across as lifelike, with a slight hint of a digital purr and a deep silky tone. The leaders sat in silence and stared at the screen. The two officers did not attempt to speak and it appeared their abductor declined permission for them to do so.

"Who do you represent, Merlin?" the president asked.

"I am not permitted by my master to say, at this time, Mr. President. I will, however tell you what our aim is."

"You have some demands you want to make?"

"No demands, Mr. President—only to state why we need the Taft."

The group remained silent, overawed by the voice, which seemed to have taken control of their nervous systems.

The president made an effort to regain his lost composure and his voice sounded strangulated. "Why does your master need the Taft?"

"The Taft is the most advanced nuclear submarine on the planet. It has admirable stealth capability and can defend itself against anything

you will try to use to destroy it. There are thirty nuclear ballistic missiles aboard, which will all be used to their fullest extent."

The group stared at the screen and at each other in horror.

∞∞

2

SPECIAL AGENT O'MALLEY

The assistant director of the FBI, James Ingram, pointed to a file on his desk. "Everything you want to know about the crew of the USS William Taft is in there."

Special Agent O'Malley reached for the file and opened it. Inside, a thick dossier of forms, each with an attached photograph of a crew member, awaited his perusal. He sifted through a few and the faces gazed up at him with benign stares, their backgrounds all laid out in specific detail on each form.

"Do you think someone on the crew might have something to do with the abduction?" O'Malley asked.

"It's highly unlikely but we need to follow up on every possible angle. This crew has operated together for eighteen months, ever since the Taft was built. None of the crew have advanced knowledge of IT systems, other than those employed for communication's purposes. Whoever hacked the master control computer is a genius. It is the most sophisticated system we have."

"So, this 'Merlin' is an AI which possesses the smarts to break any existing code or encryption. It sounds awfully like a quantum processor to me—technology which is still in its infancy," said O'-Malley.

"Anything is possible in this day and age. It has to be someone working outside the bounds of normal, localized scientific enterprise—possibly a loner. The reason for the abduction is one of revenge. Merlin did not say why or who, but it would appear someone has totally pissed off his master."

"Enough to want to wreak such a total destruction? I would say this person must be a psychopath of some sort," answered O'Malley.

"It's a very real threat. No demands have been made as of yet, but the president has been given a little time to 'think about the government's many crimes.'"

O'Malley replaced the file on the desktop. "Thirty warheads? Christ! The collateral damage is going to be huge if this maniac has his way."

"We have a huge job on our hands, Dillon. There is very little to go by but I suggest you grab your best team and find out who this psycho might be. Our only hope is to find out where this super computer of his is operating from, and then destroy it."

"Was the president given any time limit?"

"No—only that Merlin will inform us which city is to be targeted minutes before the Taft fires off a missile."

"Shit. That doesn't give us any time to evacuate people."

"Exactly. A terroristic ploy of the highest degree. Whoever Merlin's master is, the intent is to make us feel an intense fear before we are annihilated."

O'Malley stood and picked up the file. "Time is of the essence—I'll give it my best."

"Good luck. Do whatever you have to do—but let's find this bastard."

O'Malley walked back to his office, his mind in a whirl. Where should he start? Best to get his team together and discuss it. He stopped in at his secretary's office. "Shirley, ask Gabby, Roland and Diego to come to the briefing room. They need to drop whatever they're doing—it's important."

His secretary, fairly new to the job, acquiesced. "Sure, Dillon, right away."

She liked O'Malley. There seemed a brooding melancholy about the man. His dark, bushy hair and piercing blue eyes distracted her whenever they held her gaze. She deemed it a pity he was married.

Five minutes later all three team members joined O'Malley in the briefing room. He shared the bad news, moved to the white board with a dry erase marker in hand and scribbled the submarine's name at the top, and "Merlin" below it.

"We have few options here. We need to find out who Merlin's master is and hope history will be kind to us."

Gabriella Agostino, or Gabby as others called her, raised a hand. "The person is obviously a computer geek."

"Not just an ordinary geek but a super-geek, a genius who is probably a recluse of some sort and has a huge axe to grind with our government—so much so, he or she, is prepared to destroy thirty U.S. cities and millions of people to make a point," said O'Malley.

Roland McDonald, a tall, well-built man in his thirties, interjected. "Has to be a psychopath, if you ask me. There are easier ways to get even."

Diego Martinez, the quiet one in the group, smiled and nodded. "Are they sure this isn't a hoax?"

"Absolutely sure. Assistant Director Ingram was with the president this afternoon and he saw a video of the crew in the sub's control center. He also heard Merlin speak. He said it was the most sentient AI he had ever heard—sounded just like a real person, except for a slight digital purr."

McDonald pulled on his goatee. "Where do you want us to start, boss?"

O'Malley pointed to the file on the table. "You can each take a look at the crew's personal records —we can divide them up amongst us. I have my doubts if any of the crew are involved, but we can't rule it out."

He wrote MacDonald's name on the board, followed by a one-word instruction: Institute of Information Technology. "Check out the list of current and past members of the institute. See if anyone has been acknowledged for work in the area of quantum computing. Go back at least fifteen years. See if you can find anything to do with paper submissions or the like.

Next, he wrote, Gabby Agostina's name. "Read up on the requirements for quantum computers and see if you can come up with the type of hardware required for building one, Gabs. We need to pick up on the important issues of running such equipment. I don't care if you find a reputable professor who knows about such things, or whether you do your own research on the internet."

Diego received his instruction in the same way. "Do a search in the database for any IT professionals who might have committed a crime or have been charged for violations of protocol."

Martinez raised his hand. "Are we assuming the person is a US citizen?"

"I believe so. If you find nothing then widen your search to citizens of other countries, but I have a gut-feel this person lives in the U.S.A."

They divided up the crew's personal records and left the briefing room. O'Malley returned to his office and spent an hour going through the crew's details but in the end, drew a blank. Only one seaman showed positive experience with the high end of computers, Seaman Henry Davis. The lad had spent four years at MIT but his expertise fell way below the level of quantum computation. He picked up the phone and called his wife.

"Hi, honey. How's your day going?" O'Malley asked.

Janet O'Malley rattled off a long list of things that took up the most time in her day and waited for what she knew would be his next statement.

"I have to work this evening—I'll get something to eat at the deli."

She understood she could not ask him about his work and enquired as to what time he might be home.

"Something of extreme importance has come up, hon. The team and I will have to burn the midnight oil to solve a case, or people will die. I'll call you tomorrow."

*

Martinez searched the FBI's huge data base with the eye of a hawk. O'Malley knew Diego to be a hard-working, no-nonsense agent with a penchant for detail, hence the particular assignment. At twenty-seven years old and single, Diego spent almost all his time at work. His bright, intelligent eyes scanned the possible hits as the computer spewed them out. Half an hour later he pumped his fist in the air and picked up a profile with a picture. He raced to O'Malley's office.

"I think I've got something, boss."

O'Malley took the paper, squinted at the picture and scanned the profile. "Good work, Diego. I knew I could count on you to come up with something concrete. I think this might be our man. Dr. Merlin Jones. Strangely, the name rings a bell in my memory—it'll come to me."

Martinez nodded. "I believe this could be our guy. He was dismissed from the Institute of Scientific Researchers fourteen years ago because he punched the chairperson. He was charged with assault."

"The name of the computer is 'Merlin' and I think this is perhaps the biggest indication of Jones's complicity," said O'Malley.

"The police record doesn't say why he got into an altercation with the Institute's chairperson, but I'm sure Mac will come up with something," Martinez added.

At the end of the day, the team met again in the briefing room. They returned the forms which contained the crew's personal details and all three agents came up with the same answer—no one considered any of the crew to have been involved in the abduction. O'Malley gave each of the agents the opportunity to share their discoveries regarding their allocated missions.

Roland MacDonald jumped to his feet. "I had an interesting time interviewing the chairperson of the Science Institute about past members who distinguished themselves. When I pressed with regards to contributors who fell into disrepute, things really opened up. One particular person, out the four people who came to the chairperson's mind, stuck out like sore thumb—a young scientist who, at the time recently completed his doctorate. It appears he was cited in a scandal regarding the plagiarizing of work and got into an altercation with the chairperson. He ended up with an assault charge."

O'Malley, grinned. "I guess his name was Merlin Jones."

MacDonald looked surprised. "How did you know that?"

"Martinez came across him in the database. We feel he's a strong contender and might possess enough knowledge to have built the computer."

Gabby whipped out a piece of paper and jumped into the conversation. "I also have some interesting news. I spent most of the afternoon with a university professor who filled my head with the principles of quantum mechanics. I won't bore you with the details because I don't really have a head for the finer details."

MacDonald frowned. "So, what was so interesting?"

She looked down at her notes. "There are very specific requirements for the construction of a quantum computer and only a few places exist where these items can be purchased. The need of a specific material called 'nobium' for superconducting is paramount. It's used because it offers zero resistance at very low temperatures. To provide these low temperatures, a cryogenic agent is required. There is also the need for a 'pulse laser light', to place the energy levels of particles into a superposition."

"What's a superposition, professor?" Martinez asked.

Gabby shot him an annoyed glance and referred to her notes again. "Apparently according to the laws of quantum mechanics, particles become entangle with each other, you moron."

"Don't call me a moron," growled Martinez.

Martinez and Gabby often clashed over small things and on many occasions O'Malley found himself trying to keep the peace.

"Just get on with the list, Gabby—and cool down, Martinez," said O'Malley.

Gabby and Martinez stared each other down until Gabby tore her eyes away with a scowl.

"There are two other items. The first is the use of Blingalistic Pink diamonds and the second is electromagnets which are used in conjunction with the diamonds."

O'Malley raised his eyebrows. "What's a Blingalistic diamond?"

"I didn't ask, but the diamonds apparently have a capacity for the creation of what the professor called nitrogen-vacancy cavities, which promote the superposition of particles."

"Okay, okay—enough of the science lesson. Have you checked where these items can be bought and who might have purchased them?" O'Malley asked.

"I have, boss. One name, amongst the few vendor's who purchased such items, is Dr. Merlin Jones."

"We have him," stated MacDonald.

"It's been too easy. It's as though he didn't care he would be found out," said O'Malley.

Martinez contemplated the statement. "Perhaps he wants us to know he is involved. There has to be more to his story than what we know so far."

"Let's see if the internet has more to offer," said O'Malley.

He sat at the duty desk and typed in "Merlin Jones."

"Here is an old article—thirteen years ago." O'Malley read out the relevant part of the content.

"Dr. Merlin Jones, a young scientist, who was recently dismissed from the scientific Institute by his peers for apparent plagiarism, has landed in the news again. It appears his parents' home in Baltimore was mistaken for a drug operation headquarters and consequently raided by FBI SWAT team members. A smoke bomb thrown into the house by the team resulted in a fire in which Jones's parents and his younger brother, Martin, were all burned alive.

A court case ensued in which Merlin Jones, the plaintiff, sued the government for the wrongful deaths of his family members. The judge found the SWAT members not guilty and cited the event as an unfortunate accident.

Jones swore to get even and left the court in a rage."

O'Malley looked up with sudden surprise. "Now I know why I recognized the name when Diego first mentioned it. I joined the FBI police department shortly before this incident. I was the youngest member of the SWAT team involved in this incident."

∞∞

3

The USS William Taft

The news of the abduction spread quickly through the USS William Taft. The crew did not panic and placed their trust in the CO. Commander Bill Lowell and his executive officer sat together in the empty officer's wardroom. Their conversation centered on the predicament the sub's crew faced. They kept their voices a fraction above a whisper, for fear Merlin might hear their conversation through the submarine's many audio sensors.

"We have to find a way out of this situation, Bill. This madman, whoever he is, is not going to keep us hanging around once the evil deed is done," said Brown.

"I know, Ray but we need to concentrate on an escape plan which will save the entire crew, plus prevent the AI from releasing our D5 missiles."

"I've been racking my brains but each time something materializes, I see a downside to it," said the XO.

"I have an idea. We need to find a way of decommissioning the firing, selector switches on each silo. That way Merlin will not realize the circuits of each mechanism cannot be closed."

Brown contemplated the possibility. "That will take some doing. I think we need to talk to Peterson and see how it could be done without drawing Merlin's attention."

"Peterson has worked on plenty of firing systems in his time. If anyone knows a way, he will," said Lowell.

"On a second thought, why should we worry about the AI picking up the action? What can it actually do?"

"Make things extremely uncomfortable for us. Remember—it doesn't need us to complete its mission."

Brown gave a gesture of resignation. "That's a thought I don't want to entertain."

"Nor I, but we must bear it in mind. Whatever we come up with must be foolproof."

"When will you talk to Peterson?"

"Right away. We don't know how much time we have. At least Ops knows our present situation and they must be doing everything in their power to help."

*

Ten minutes later, Lowell met with his chief engineering officer. Peterson joined the Taft as head of the engineering department a week before its maiden voyage. His cool and businesslike demeanor made him a great go-to person for any of the sub's engineering problems and he knew all the electronic circuitry schematics off by heart.

"Would it be possible to decommission the firing, selector switches on each of the missile tubes without alerting the AI?"

"I think we might be able to, sir. We would need to remove the cover plate at the base of each tube, which will give us direct access to the firing mechanism circuitry. The switches, unfortunately are solid units, so—the only way to prevent the circuit from closing is to cut the live wire to the switch."

Lowell tried to picture the concept. "Is there not a malfunction-detection process which alerts the main control computer?"

"There is, but it will only detect the malfunction at the time of actual firing. If we can decommission all the switches, there is no way Merlin can repair them."

"The more I think about it the more I fancy our chances of pulling it off. How many of your guys are competent on these electronics?" Lowell asked.

"There are four techs who will know what they are doing. I wish we had thirty for the task—we would be able to do all thirty tubes simultaneously, but I'm afraid we don't have such a luxury," said Peterson.

"Can't we instruct capable people to do it?"

"It's a risk, skipper. One slip, and the switch could just as well close while being worked on. I'm sure I have no need to tell you what the consequences would be."

"I get your drift," retorted Lowell. "Get your four guys to meet with us at 1400 hours in the wardroom. I'll get the camera temporarily disabled."

"Aye, aye, sir." Peterson gave a short salute and left.

An hour later the four technicians made their way into the missile compartment. Ray Brown, the executive officer, followed them into the brightly lit corridor. Brown, the last man in placed a towel over the camera, situated above the compartment's entrance. The cameras might become a problem but they didn't know how connected Merlin might be to the electronic gadgets on the sub. Each tech went to work with an urgency. The panels on the side of the tubes contained dozens of small hex bolts, which needed to be removed with a power driver before the gas generator electronics could be exposed. The Taft, like its predecessors, employed the cold-launch missile system, which required the initial stage of the projectile's flight to be initiated by gas for clearance of the launch tube. After that, the first stage rocket motor took over to propel the missile upward and onward.

Several minutes passed before the removal of the first cover plate. The other three plates followed in short duration. The technicians checked the wiring diagram on the inside of their particular cover and identified the live feed to the firing switch but without warning, the lights in the compartment extinguished. One of the techs pulled out a flashlight and held it in his teeth while he continued to work. Ray Brown frowned in surprise at the sudden disappearance of overhead light. Moments later the breathable air began to diminish. His lungs struggled for each breath and small pinpricks of light flashed before his eyes before he fainted. The missile compartment's airtight door could not be opened and the five men collapsed on the walkway between the silos. All four techs succumbed in quick order—silence reigned.

Commander Bill Lowell looked through the door's small glass window and observed the sudden darkness within the missile compartment. In place of the extinguished overhead light he noticed the feint glow of a flashlight, but it too, went out. A notion of fear swept Lowell's mind as he took hold of the manual lever, which operated the door lock-mechanism, and applied all his strength to it. The lever did not budge. The electronic lock prevented the action.

"Quick sailor, give me a hand," he shouted. The fire-control technician grabbed the lever in conjunction with Lowell and the two of them made a valiant attempt to force it downward, but to no avail.

"They've been locked in. The AI must have picked up on our plan somehow," said the commander.

They stood outside the compartment and gazed at the door, but nothing could be done. The commander shut his eyes and prayed for a miracle, which never came. He looked at the three fire-control technicians and pointed to the door. "Stay here and listen for the electronic lock to disengage—I'm going to the control room."

Lowell ran along the corridor and through missile control. He took the stairs to the bridge in three leaps. On the screen above the steering section a message awaited him.

"What are you trying to do, Commander Lowell?"

He spoke to the officer of the deck. "Switch on the master control computer's audio. I want to speak to Merlin—I want to hear its voice."The OOD did as he asked and a distinct hum emanated from the speaker in the ceiling.

"I must ask you the same question," said Lowell.

"You and your crew are up to something, Commander. The camera in the missile tube compartment has been covered. Did you think I would not know about it?"

Lowell lied. "I don't know what you're talking about."

Merlin gave an ominous chuckle. *"Oh, you certainly do, Commander. You have been planning something for the last few hours and I think I know what it is."*

"What are you accusing me off, Merlin?"

"You were obviously trying to disable the firing switches in the missile tubes. I am going to open the door to the compartment in half an hour and you will order your men to remove the rag from the camera lens. The entire missile area will be off limits to everyone."

"What about my men?" Lowell ventured.

"I imagine they will be dead, Commander. Humans cannot live without air, as you well know."

Lowell felt a rage within. "You killed my men?"

"No, you killed your own men, Commander Lowell. Let this serve as a warning—it's useless to fight me. I am in complete control."

Lowell looked at the speaker grid in the ceiling and lost his sense of hope. With head hung low, the commander vowed to get even with Merlin's master and he turned to walk back to the missile compartment. A few minutes later, he waited with the three fire-control technicians at the missile tube compartment door. A half hour passed before they heard the click of the lock as it disengaged.

Air from the missile control center rushed in to replace the vacuum and Lowell, with his heart in his boots, looked into the compartment. The bodies of his men lay on the mezzanine walkway, some spread-eagled and others slumped against the missile silos.

He wanted to cry. The weight of the lost lives hung like heavy anvils and he felt responsible for sending five good men to their deaths. Ray Brown's expression would be etched into his mind for the remainder of his existence.

"Take these bodies to the sickbay. Ask the duty corpsman to confine them in the cryogenic storage facility and tell him I will be in my stateroom."

Back in his quarters, Lowell considered the crews options. Merlin would kill them all in the end. The only worthwhile action would end their lives. He knew they needed to destroy the Taft before Merlin deployed its lethal cargo. The independent duty corpsman arrived to discuss the commander's reason for continued storage of the dead bodies, as opposed to a sea burial. They could speak freely as no audio sensors existed in Lowell's stateroom.

"The reason for the use of cryogenic storage is the strong possibility of the Taft being sunk with its entire compliment. The U.S. authorities will make an attempt at finding our sub and recovering all the bodies. It's an extremely negative thought, but we need to plan for the worst scenario," said Lowell.

The duty corpsman responded with a tone of alarm. "But sir, why do you think the AI will destroy us? It doesn't need us for anything and we certainly won't be able to pose any threat."

Lowell countered. "The very reason for it having no need of us will seal our fate. If Merlin doesn't destroy us, the U.S. Navy will, and if they don't—we'll have to do it ourselves. "

"How do you propose we destroy the Taft, sir?" the corpsman asked.

"I need to talk to the weapons officer. Please inform him to join me in my quarters—we will figure something out."

∞∞

4

The Investigation begins in Earnest

O'Malley and the team sat around the coffee table in review of their investigation.

"So you actually met this infamous Dr. Jones?" Gabby asked.

O'Malley reflected on his past experience. "I can't say I met him, but I did get a look at him on our day in court. There were five us. We were called out to bust a supposed dangerous drug operation in an upmarket neighborhood. The problem lay with the address the dispatch gave us—it was the wrong house. Our lead agent threw a smoke grenade through an open window, which somehow caused a problem and the house went up in flames before we could do anything."

"Did you try to rescue the occupants?" Mac-Donald asked.

"We rushed in, but the smoke prevented us from finding them. They had taken fright and hid in the basement. It was an old house and the wooden floors burned quickly, which caused a cave-in and buried the family below. We thought the house was empty."

"You were acquitted of wrong doing, though?"

"The judge said the dispatch was at fault in giving us the wrong address, but the department lawyers were good and it ended up as one of those contingencies, which throw reasonable doubt over the circumstance. The department offered compensation for the loss of the house, but nothing further."

Martinez made a valid comment. "It's possible Dr. Jones has a vendetta against the FBI as well—not only the government."

O'Malley considered the implication. "He could, indeed—the names of all those involved are common record."

"Which means you might have a target on your back," said Gabby.

"It's possible. Two of the other SWAT team members have since died. There are three of us left."

Martinez left the coffee table and sat down at the briefing room computer. "Do you remember the name of the judge?"

"It's the same judge who granted us an injunction in my last big investigation to do with the memory sweep episode—Steinbeck," said O'Malley.

Martinez typed in the name and clicked on the relevant website. His eyes widened in surprise. "You're not going to believe this."

"What?" O'Malley asked.

Martinez read out a section of the article.

"Judge Marvin Steinbeck died yesterday in an aircraft accident. The private jet, in which he and three other family members were traveling, crashed into a heavily wooded area outside Nebraska at approximately two p.m. The cause is unknown but could have been a malfunction of the craft's instrumentation."

O'Malley looked dumbfounded. MacDonald ventured his opinion. "It could have been a genuine accident."

"Or it could have been a computer takeover of the craft's instruments," added Martinez.

"If Jones is using Merlin to clear the slate on the death of his family he'll be targeting the remaining members of the SWAT team. The two guys, beside myself, are now field agents in the department. I'll check up on them," said O'Malley.

In the meantime, what do you want us to concentrate on?" asked MacDonald.

"We need to find out where Jones is hiding himself. To start with, let's concentrate on trying to pick up his trail after the court case. He needed to make some sort of a living. Time would have been spent on continuing his quantum computer research, and my bet is he might have changed his name," said O'Malley.

The meeting ended and O'Malley went home for a short rest. After thirty-six hours, he needed to sleep.

*

On arrival he found Janet in the kitchen. "Hi, honey. It was a rough night—I'm hungry and tired."

"I'll fix you up some bacon and eggs, sweetheart," she said.

"Thanks, hon. Steven get off to school okay?"

"Yes, with the usual reluctance."

"He's growing up," offered O'Malley.

Janet busied herself in preparing a quick meal for him. "I think he's withdrawing more than usual, though. I think Fallon's death is becoming a greater reality as he gets to know girls more."

"It's been two and half years since she died and he'll be sixteen soon. I think he is beginning to realize what we as parents went through with the loss of our daughter."

Fallon O'Malley and a friend, victims of a hit-and-run on their school prom night, both passed away on the night of the fatal accident. The event placed a strain on O'Malley's marriage and they agreed to a second round of counseling to prevent a complete breakdown.

"Will you be able to make the counseling session tonight?" Janet asked.

"I can't make it, hon, I'm sorry. Ingram has several teams involved in this latest investigation and we all have to be on our toes. I can't say much, but there's a madman on the loose trying to kill people and he must be stopped."

"I understand, Dillon. It's just frustrating for me to make headway in resolving our issues and then your job intervenes."

O'Malley gave her a hurt look. "I understand you're frustrated, Jan..."

Janet teared up and continued to fry the eggs. She turned her back on him, an action she always took when they could not see eye to eye.

"I'm doing my best, honey. This case I'm on has national consequences and if we don't catch the perpetrator, many people will die."

She gestured exasperation with one hand but didn't turn around. He knew it would be useless to continue any form of placation or self-justification. Janet completed the breakfast and dished the meal onto a plate, which she plonked down in front of him.

"Let's not fight," she said. "We're both tired—I'll go to the counseling session on my own."

O'Malley nodded and tucked into the eggs. She would take a few hours to get over her frustration and when he returned he hoped they would be able to sit down and have a talk. He knew he needed to overcome the guilt with regard to his daughter's death. He always felt it to be his fault because he never cautioned Fallon about leaving the prom with friends in a car, but no amount of guilt on his behalf would bring her back.

Two hours later O'Malley woke up and stumbled through to the bathroom. After a face wash and shave he felt better, ready for coffee. He called for Janet but received no answer and concluded she must have gone out to the shop on the corner. He emptied the old coffee out into the sink, made a fresh brew and sat at the kitchen table to make a few calls. The issue of Judge Steinbeck's death still rattled him and he needed to make sure his old comrades were safe. The first call to Robin Schofield's cell, ended with him leaving a message on the answering service. The second call on the department's land line to Schofield's office had the auto system directed his enquiry back to the FBI. He waited for a few moments before a woman came on the line.

"Can I help you?" she asked.

O'Malley identified himself and asked for Robin. He received news, which sent a chill down his spine.

"I'm afraid Robin was killed last night, Special Agent, O'Malley."

O'Malley felt the cold hand of death on his shoulder. "Can you tell me how he died?"

"Cause of death is still to be determined," she said. "But it appears to have been an accident of some sort.

O'Malley thanked her and hung up. Perspiration popped out on his brow and started to course down his forehead. He needed to get hold of the remaining member of the defunct SWAT team if the man was still alive. He called the number again and left another message. Charley Bader might still be in one piece.

*

Back in his office, he received the return call from Charley Bader. The agent could not answer the phone at the time O'Malley called due to an unexpected meeting with one of his informants. The man arranged to meet with Charley but on his way to the rendezvous Charley's vehicle broke down, which made him twenty minutes late.

O'Malley related the specifics of the case regarding Jones and the dangers it posed for them. Bader expressed surprise and said he would be more aware of his surroundings, in particular any situations where a computer might have a form of control. O'Malley closed off the conversation and walked to the briefing room, where he found Gabby at the computer.

"Where are the others?" O'Malley asked.

"Out following up on leads," she said. "I'm just doing some research before I go out. He told her about Robin Schofield's death and his call to Bader.

She whistled. "I perceive Merlin is extremely active. I suggest you don't go anywhere alone until this is all sorted out, Dillon."

Perhaps you're right, Gabs. You can team up with me. What are you working on?"

"I'm checking on Dr. Merlin Jones's last known whereabouts. It appears he rented an old, deserted warehouse in the Bronx area after the clash with the Institute."

"You got an address?"

She smiled. "Of course, boss—you up for a jaunt?"

"Let's go," he said.

They took the black Chevy allocated to O'Malley and drove to the Bronx. Ninety minutes later, they pulled into the grounds of a deserted warehouse on a small parcel of ground. The building appeared to be deserted and unused for some time.

"You sure this is the right place?" he asked.

Gabby looked at some notes on her phone. "This is it. Let's check it out—let me go first."

O'Malley allowed Gabby to lead the way. He knew her to be a formidable force in any difficult circumstance. Five years in Iraq and now five years with the FBI had honed her investigative skills and also her penchant for conflict. The door to the main building opened easily, which indicated the landlord still kept up the maintenance. The floors were swept clean, but the lack of equipment suggested the absence of renters.

Gabby pulled her Glock from its holster and moved with cat-like agility into the area, ready to face any unknown foe. O'Malley drew his weapon and covered her back. The high windows allowed a minimum amount of light, but enough for them to see the entire floor clearly. An electrical panel on the far wall caught their eye.

"Let's see if there's power to the building," said Gabby. A closed door in the adjacent wall drew their attention.

"You check out what's behind that door. I'll see if there's any power," said O'Malley.

They separated and O'Malley walked carefully toward the panel. He looked up to the corners of the two interlocking walls and saw a tiny camera pointed at him. He expected the building would have security. Vandals were often a problem for the landlords of empty buildings. Gabby reached the door and opened it.

"It's a small storeroom—empty," she shouted.

O'Malley stopped in front of the panel and gazed at the contents. A large main switch rested in the "off" position. He reached out his hand to flip the switch, but Gabby shouted at him. "Don't touch it, Dillon."

O'Malley pulled back his hand and as he did so the entire electrical panel ignited in a flame, which scorched his eyebrows and singed his hair. For a moment he couldn't see and fell backward onto the floor. His Glock landed a yard away on the ground. Gabby shrieked his name and ran toward him. The electrical panel erupted in another bright flash of light and for a moment, she hesitated to go near as flames shot out of the board and burned it to a crisp. Gabby overcame her fear and ran to where O'Malley lay. She shook him and he sat upright, his hands over his eyes.

"I can't see anything," he said.

"Just give it a minute, Dillon. Don't rub your eyes."

A moment later O'Malley could see again. "That was a close call. Thanks for the warning, Gabs."

"You're welcome, boss. Just as well we decided to work together."

O'Malley got to his feet with Gabby's help and he stood for a short while, regaining his balance. The burned out electrical panel still exuded puffs of smoke. "My guess—Merlin. This was no accident. Do you see the camera up on the wall?"

Gabby looked up and squinted in the semi-darkness. "I see it."

O'Malley shouted at the camera. "You bastard, Jones. You won't get me that easily."

They left the building with a new awareness. Merlin's eyes seemed to be everywhere and O'Malley could feel the cold presence of his potential assassin. Back at the office, a message on his office phone awaited him. "Call Charley Bader."

He pulled out his cell phone to key in the number. The answering service greeted him, but instead of Charley's voice a silky, purr of an assimilated voice, the type used by modern supercomputers, spoke into his ear:

"I have taken care of your friend, Special Agent O'Malley. You may have escaped my first attempt to get you, but you won't get off so lightly the next time."

∞∞

5

A Second meeting with Merlin.

President Barrow sifted through the presidential mail with a critical eye. Correspondence from corporations, senators and congressmen each with an objection to some law or executive decision made by the Barrow administration, arrived daily. The letters he looked forward to and enjoyed the most, however, came from children. Once in a while, a third or fifth grader would write him on a subject close to their heart, or to thank him for being such a nice man. These communications always made his day and made him feel like the patriarch of the nation.

Eli popped his head around the door. "Are you busy, boss?"

"Just the usual grind, Eli—come in."

"Actually, can you come to the operations room?"

"Something important?"

"Yes, sir. It's to do with the Taft. The AI is coming online in a minute or so. It wants to talk to you."

The president shot out of his chair. "I have a bad feeling about this, Eli. Has there been any new information from any of the intelligence departments?"

"I spoke to Assistant Director Ingram earlier today and he said Merlin's powers are far reaching. The AI has threatened those on the case and it would appear this Merlin Jones has a vendetta against the U.S government, the judiciary and certain members of the FBI."

They walked down the corridor to the operations room and the chief of staff explained the past incident, which involved Merlin Jones's family. Eli told the president about the deaths of Judge Steinbeck and the two FBI agents involved in the original SWAT operation.

"This is uncanny and scary," said the president. "How safe are our classified communications?"

"Judging by Merlin's ability to have hacked into our latest sub technology with the most difficult encryption codes in the world—I'd say nothing to do with electronics or the cyber world is safe."

"Good God, Eli—what are we going to do?"

They entered the operations room and sat down in front of the huge TV screen. A minute later the image of the USS William Taft's control room materialized. The audio boomed through the twin speakers on either side of the TV.

"Greetings, Mr. President. I trust you are well. By now you will know my master is Dr. Merlin Jones. This bit of trivia is of little consequence because you will not find him until he is ready to reveal himself. Dr. Jones has much planned for you in the short time before we release the Taft's payload. I must tell you the crew of the USS William Taft tried to disable the nuclear firing system aboard the vessel—this was a mistake for which a few have paid dearly."

The overhead camera in the control room's ceiling swiveled to reveal Commander Lowell, who stood against a wall of instruments with his hands behind his back. The look on the commander's face revealed a sullen defiance, but the slight hang in the head suggested a measure of defeat.

The president burst out in anger. "If you have hurt any of the crew, by God, you'll pay for it, Merlin."

The AI chuckled. *"I understand your frustration, Mr. President, but you must realize one thing: I hold all the cards. The US military is now like a dog without any teeth. There is nothing you can do to stop me."*

"Can I talk to Commander Lowell?"

"You can, Mr. President. He can hear you, but I don't think he will have much to say."

"Are you okay, Bill?" asked the president.

"Considering the situation, I'm okay, Mr. President."

"Are the crew okay?"

"I am sad to report that five brave members of our crew are dead, sir."

"I'm sorry to hear that, Bill. Make sure that no one else does anything to earn a similar fate, however, you must be aware we cannot allow the Taft to fire even one of its missiles. You realize, of course, we have every possible resource looking for you."

Lowell hesitated and then gave a wan smile. "I understand, sir. We will do our best to stay cheerful. The crew understands what will happen when you discover the Taft's position."

"Thank you, Bill. Know that you have our deepest sympathies regarding your unfortunate position. We will inform every one of the crew's family members, as to what's going on."

"Thank you, sir. I'll let the crew know."

The president smiled for a brief second before his brow creased into a deep frown. "So, Merlin. Are you willing to tell me when you will start to reign terror on our nation?"

Merlin hesitated before giving his answer. *"The preamble up to, and before the use of the missiles, will keep you and your administration very busy but I will let you know the details when the Taft is in the optimum position for the final countdown to your destruction."*

Barrow leaned forward in his seat. "Is there nothing that we can do to make right what the previous administration got wrong?"

"There is only retribution, Mr. President. Merlin out."

The screen went blank and the operations room fell silent. The president looked at his Chief of Staff. "Bill Lowell is a brave and resourceful man. He knows their fate is sealed. I believe he will do everything in his power to destroy the Taft if we don't get to her first.

*

Bill Lowell looked across the table at the Taft's Chief Engineering Officer, William Peterson, and sensed the sadness in the man's heart. Peterson recently received the news of the latest edition to their family, a ten-pound baby boy named Charles, a few days prior to the abduction of the Taft. He would never get to meet his new son. The Commander's stateroom seemed like a modern mausoleum to the two men as they deliberated the fate of their submarine.

"You think this plan will work without initial detection?" Lowell asked.

"I believe it's possible. The silver oxide battery used in the ignition and propulsion system of a Black Shark torpedo can be rigged to explode— remember the theory on how the Scorpion sank all those years ago?" Peterson asked.

Lowell nodded. "One of our case studies in submarine disasters. It's thought the battery might have malfunctioned and set the torpedo off in its tube."

"If we can get someone to rig up cables from the battery to the warhead's trigger system, the torpedo could be exploded manually."

"Is there no detection device in the torpedo tubes which might alert the AI to someone fiddling with the battery?"

"None. The Taft might be the most advanced computerized SSBN in the U.S. Navy, but they didn't feel the need to cover every square inch of the systems with sensors."

"There is a camera in the compartment, though," said Lowell.

"There is, but it's in a place where access to the system's batteries are not easily viewable."

"How long will it take for the Taft to sink?"

Peterson considered the answer. "It's hard to say but at a guess, at least twelve minutes. We only have to detonate one torpedo."

Lowell chewed on his top lip for a moment. "The act will need to be in conjunction with a routine clean of the compartment, so as not to raise any suspicion. You'll need to arrange with the fire-control techs, who do the cleaning."

"I believe the schedule has it for 2400 hours. The techs move in with cleaning materials, plus an engineer to check the system—they have the ideal cover to perform the task. I will explain to them exactly how it must be done," said Peterson.

Lowell looked at his watch. "We have twelve hours before it can be accomplished. The president made it clear we are on our own. They are doing everything in their power to locate the Taft, but it is highly probable they will fail."

"It seems unreal—in twelve and half hours, we will all be dead," ventured Peterson.

"A completely necessary sacrifice, I'm afraid. Just think what one of these ballistic missiles will do to a city. Millions of people will die."

"I know it's unavoidable. I feel an anger toward the designers of the Taft, though. They should have foreseen the possibility of an outside source hacking the master control computer and perhaps given us a system or two not under its control."

"The price we pay for modern technology. Put it out of your mind, Lieutenant. We have a job to do and it's the last contribution we'll make to the human cause—so, let's make sure it's done properly. Go and talk to your men."

"Aye, aye, sir. We will succeed," said Peterson. He saluted and left the stateroom.

Lowell opened a desk drawer and removed an oblong metal box. He picked up a ballpoint pen and started to write a note to his wife and family. The note did not contain any tearfully-sentimental overtures but a short account of the events which led up to the Taft's abduction and the crew's plight. He told his wife he loved her with all his heart. He thanked her for the years of support for his career and putting up with his long stints at sea. He also thanked her for producing four wonderful children to fill their lives with love and delight. He wrote a short note for each child and then added on a separate sheet a codicil to his will, allocating the most recent material requirements of sentimental value to various family members.

*

The Chief of Navy Operations, Admiral Jane Carlton, rose from her chair and moved to the whiteboard in the operations room. The other members of the joint chiefs looked on with solemn contemplation as she picked up the dry eraser and drew a rough picture of the North American continent with its two sea boards on either side. The president sat at the back of the room with a grim and dispassionate expression.

The question the president posed raised a contemplative atmosphere in the otherwise gloom of the room. "Where in the seas would be the optimum position for a sub to position itself for a strike on the largest U.S. cities?"

The admiral pointed to three spots; one at the entrance to the of Gulf of Mexico, the second, four thousand miles off the east coast in the Atlantic and the third, a few thousand miles off the west coast in the Pacific.

"The extreme range of the ballistic missile is four thousand two hundred and thirty miles. We can't be sure the Taft will stay at this range, but my guess is it will be slightly within this distance. There is too much navy traffic closer in, which increases the risk of detection," she said.

The president raised his hand. "What speed does this ballistic missile travel at, Jane?"

"It's extremely quick, sir—18000 mph."

"Good Lord—that gives us very little time to respond once the missile breaks surface," said Eli Marion.

The admiral nodded. "We don't have anything that can match it for speed, so it cannot be shot down. It's also guided by the latest inertial guidance navigation system, which will make sure it hits the target with pin-point accuracy."

The Chief of Air Operations came up with a relevant question. "When the missile breaks surface would it not reveal the Taft's position? If we have enough airpower flying overhead in these three positions, we may get lucky."

"That's a great suggestion, Arnold. If we can strike the Taft after it's released its first missile, we will greatly lessen the collateral damage," said the president.

The Chief of the Marine Corp came up with a suggestion. "Should we not assume Jones' strategy would be to hit the cities with the largest populations and make plans to evacuate these?"

"A logistical nightmare, Gordon," said the president.

The general did not back down but pressed the point. "I realize it would be impossible to evacuate an entire city in hours, but surely we can get people out of the city centers?"

"You have a point." The president turned and spoke to an aide, who sat beside him. "Set up an immediate meeting with Homeland security. If they feel this is a viable option it would need to be set up without delay."

The aide hived off and the president addressed the Chief of Air Operations. "Set up a grid reconnaissance group to fly over these three areas, covering as wide an area as possible. Mobilize the new

B21's if need be and keep them in the air until we can achieve a sighting."

The meeting ended and everyone went their separate ways. The secretary of State confronted him in the corridor on the way to the oval office. "Sir, I have just received a call from the Russian Ambassador. They have heard about the Taft."

∞∞

6

The Investigation gathers Momentum.

O'Malley closed his eyes and placed his free hand on his brow. The phone, still clutched in the other hand, remained glued to the side of his face. All he could muster were three words. "Oh God, no."

Gabby stared at him with concern. "What is it, Dillon?"

He opened his eyes and replaced the phone on its cradle. "Bader is dead. That leaves me as Merlin's final target for the SWAT team."

"How did he die?" Gabby asked.

"I don't know yet. Somehow Merlin is able to connect to our phones. The AI left a message on Bader's phone to say he got Bader, and although I escaped at the warehouse, I won't be so lucky in the future."

"Maybe you should bow out, Dillon. Go and hide yourself and your family somewhere and let us finish this off."

"Absolutely not," growled O'Malley. "I'm not going to let a computer get the better of me. I can't hide myself away when there's so much at stake. I need to protect my family, though."

O'Malley picked up the phone to call the assistant director of the FBI, James Ingram. After relating the details of his narrow escape, he asked that his family be afforded protection in a safe place.

"I'll call Janet right away to pick up Steven from school. They'll be ready if you can arrange for a car to take them to her mother's place on the outskirts of Baltimore," said O'Malley.

The assistant director acquiesced. "What about you, Dillon? Shouldn't you also think of going into hiding?"

O'Malley repeated what he told Gabby. "I'll stay on the case until we resolve it, or Merlin blows us to Kingdom come."

He turned to Gabby. "Call in Martinez and MacDonald. We need to do some serious planning."

A call to Janet followed. She wanted to know the purpose. "Honey, I don't have time to explain why you and Steven must get out of D.C. It's to do with this latest case I'm on and we need to anticipate, that because of my involvement, my immediate family might be in some danger. I'll explain more when I see you."

She wanted to know when he would come to see them. "I don't know, sweetheart—as soon as it's humanly possible, but right now, I have to find the madman I told you about."

With a reminder of his need to be safe and how she hated this part of his job, Janet relented and said she would pick Steven up from school.

An hour later, the team met in the briefing room and O'Malley related his experience regarding the warehouse incident.

"We need to brainstorm the many ways Merlin can attack us and at the same time, discover what happened to Jones after the court case."

MacDonald looked surprised. "Do you think Merlin will attack the whole team and not just you?"

"This is one smart-ass computer we're dealing with. Don't forget it's not an ordinary AI. Quantum computing can deal with a thousand times more data than any ordinary processor. We must assume Merlin will know everything about us—everything that's on record."

"Any news as to what's happening with the submarine?" Gabby asked.

"Ingram says Merlin communicated with the president today and said that once the sub was in the right position, they would begin the strikes."

He stepped up to the whiteboard. "Let's see how many possible dangers exist as we go about our investigation."

Martinez leaned back in the chair and placed his hands behind his head. "You're talking about any situation where a computer might have access to change the normal scope of a system's operation?"

"Exactly. Don't forget this is no ordinary computer. Try to stretch your imaginations a little," said O'Malley.

"We already know about electrical distribution boards and switches," added Gabby.

"Moveable bridges—where traffic is stopped for boats to pass through waterways," said MacDonald. "I have it on good authority there are almost thirty such bridges scattered around the waterways of New York."

O'Malley wrote it down on the white board. "Get on the internet and find where every one of these bridges are, Mac. You can make a list for each of us."

"Electric train crossings?" ventured Gabby.

"Good thinking, Gabs. Merlin will more than likely have already hacked into several GPS satellites—let's not diminish the AI's ability to track us on the roads. Although it may be a bit of a long shot for it to catch us approaching level crossings, anything is possible."

"What about the electrical components in our vehicles?" Martinez suggested.

"That's something we haven't thought of," said O'Malley. He wrote it down. "I see there could be a problem in the ability for us to detect Merlin's every action."

"Commuter trains," offered MacDonald. "We often use the subways to avoid heavy traffic on certain days."

"Okay," said O'Malley. "Enough for the time being. If any of you think of something more, just send a text. We need to get on with our search for Jones. Be careful out there."

Martinez and MacDonald left the room. Gabby shot O'Malley an enquiring glance. "Are you still wanting to team up, boss?"

"Sure thing. Give me a moment and we can get on with our follow up—I need to pee."

*

Ten minutes later O'Malley and Gabby drove to a shop in Manhattan. Their investigation showed the owner of the warehouse also ran a deli. It could be helpful to find out what the landlord knew about Jones. The deli turned out to be a small narrow shop, which extended down into the depths of the building with the counter on one side and a single row of tables, against the opposite wall. The owner, a Greek with pockmarked facial skin, looked at them with suspicion when they pulled out their badges.

O'Malley made the purpose for the visit known. He pulled out an old picture of Jones taken from the FBI archives and thrust it at the deli owner. "You rented a warehouse to this man. Do you know what happened after he moved his equipment out?"

The man squinted at the picture. "Oh yes, Mr. Jones—I remember him. It's been about five years since his lease was up. He did not renew it."

"Do you know what he used the building for?"

The deli owner gave the question some consideration. "I'm not really sure, but it featured computer applications of some sort."

"When he moved out, did he leave a forward address for mail?" Gabby asked.

"It was a Post Office box number if I remember, but I never received anything to be forwarded. He also paid cash for everything."

"Do you have the box number available?"

The deli owner told them to wait while he extracted the information from his files, which he kept in a small box-like office at the back of the narrow room. Armed with the information, Gabby did a search of the number to find the local location of the post office and they took off in the Chevy for Murdock Avenue. Due to heavy traffic, it took twenty-five minutes of careful driving before they pulled up in a no-parking zone outside the post office. He hung the FBI official card on the inside rearview mirror, they climbed the steps to the entrance and went straight to the information desk.

O'Malley produced his badge and the clerk called her supervisor to help.

"We need to check if this box is still rented to this person." He gave Jones' name and the box number.

The supervisor asked them to follow him into a room which contained walls of safety deposit boxes and within seconds they found the box in question. "Open it up," said O'Malley.

The supervisor inserted the key, turned it and pulled the door open. A loud bang emanated from the confines of the box, followed by the sound of a gas under compression. The blast blew the door off its hinges and the supervisor fell over backward. A strong, acrid smell of toxic fumes, visible by a greenish-yellow tinge of color, filled the room.

O'Malley acted with speed. He took a deep breath and grabbed the supervisor by the collar of his jacket and dragged the inert body toward the exit of the room. Gabby followed behind, her one hand held over her eyes and they fell into the corridor, which led to the main post office admin area. People screamed and fled the building in fear while the two agents dragged the supervisor between them to safety. The fumes filled the safety deposit room within seconds of the blast and billowed out into the rest of the rooms. The two FBI agents dragged the supervisor into the main service area and fell to their knees with violent coughing and choking. For a few seconds, silence reigned; then a distant siren could be heard and with it, sounds of people calling out to each other. A dark green smoke filled all the rooms and O'Malley knew they needed to get to the street with as much speed as possible.

"Quickly, Gabby. We must get out of here—help me drag the supervisor to the front entrance."

Gabby responded with a series of coughs and splutters but grabbed the back of the supervisor's jacket and together they pulled the unconscious form through the front entrance, to fall down the stairs, onto the side walk. People gathered around them and rendered assistance. Someone turned the supervisor over onto his back. The person shouted, "Does anyone know CPR?"

Two people came forward and started to work on the supervisor. O'Malley got to his feet but could not stop coughing. His head felt as though it would split apart and a sudden lack of balance caused him to fall to his knees. Strong arms grabbed him from behind and lifted him back onto his feet. "Take it easy, sir—we're here to help you."

O'Malley opened his eyes as a paramedic assisted him toward the backdoors of their service vehicle and another helped him onto a bunk situated within.

"What happened?" asked the paramedic.

O'Malley struggled to speak. "A strong toxic gas."

Another cough-spurt prevented any further words, but he gave the paramedic enough information to start a procedure. The application of oxygen cleared his airway and immediate relief came as his lungs returned to normal. His eyes burned as a solution, applied with some vigor, helped to remove the toxic agent from the sclera of his eyes. A few moments later, he glanced across and saw Gabby lying on the bunk opposite him. She, too, received the same treatment and after a while her coughing subsided. O'Malley needed to know the condition of the supervisor. He produced his badge and removed the oxygen mask to speak.

"How is the person we dragged out of the building doing?"

The paramedic shook his head. "Didn't make it, I'm afraid."

An icy grip took hold of O'Malley's heart. He looked across at Gabby. "You okay, Gabs?"

"I'll live, boss," she said.

"The supervisor didn't make it. That little treat was meant for me, but I never gave the possibility a thought."

She understood the real meaning of his words. "Don't beat yourself over the head, Dillon. You couldn't have known."

"We should have been more aware."

Gabby raised herself off the bunk and moved over to him. She took his head in both her hands and stared into his eyes.

"Listen to me, boss. You couldn't have known this was going to happen. It's a tragedy that someone's dead, but remember—Merlin Jones is responsible. Concentrate your energy on finding him and putting him away forever." Her voice displayed a firm tone.

The paramedic climbed into the back of the vehicle and shut the doors. "We're taking you to the hospital for a quick checkup, but you both should be fine."

The emergency vehicle pulled away from the curb and entered the traffic. O'Malley felt a strange detachment and closed his eyes.

An hour later they were both discharged. Mac-Donald arrived at the hospital with the Chevy and after a brief discussion, with regard to the incident they drove back toward the J. Edgar Hoover building in silence.

MacDonald made a statement. "Martinez has made an important discovery."

∞∞

7

The Crew of the USS William Taft.

Under the instruction of Chief Engineer Peterson, Petty Officer Hunt called in four of his most competent weapon techs and laid out the plan of the Taft's destruction.

"You must understand our plight. As far as the AI is concerned the Taft's crew is totally expendable. I am going to tell you the truth about our position and why we must act—if we don't offer ourselves as the proverbial sacrifice, many millions of people will die. I think everyone knows why the sub was abducted. The thirty Tridents on board are going to be used against our country. Our own families, depending where we live, are at extreme risk."

One of the techs responded with a question. "What if the Navy or Air Operations discover us first?"

"Same result," said Hunt. "They already have an executive order to blow us out of the water."

"So we're damned if we do and damned if we don't?" the tech retorted.

Hunt composed himself. He could feel the tension rising. "I would rather be seen as a hero by sending the Taft to the bottom of the ocean, than allow this demon to destroy millions of Americans. I wish there was an alternative, but there isn't."

The group of three techs and one engineer stood in silent contemplation of his words. Another tech spoke out. "I'm inclined to agree, sir. We can't allow the destruction of our countrymen and families to happen. What is it you want us to do?"

Hunt breathed a sigh of relief. "Thank you for your trust."

He proceeded to outline the plan of using cables attached to the torpedo's battery terminals to form a circuit for the detonation of the warhead. The four techs would replace the usual cleaning crew and enter the torpedo room at the scheduled time.

*

Commander Lowell watched the control room instrumentation like a hawk. The sonar supervisor and two planesmen, despite the shut-out by Merlin, also continued to stare at the screens and dials. They watched each bank of sonar consoles, one for the starboard side and the other for port activity, with a keen intensity. The supervisor analyzed each enhancement along with its flow of sonic indictors, which appeared against the green backdrops on the screens, with great concern. The chief sonar operator kept his ears glued to the headphones for sounds brought back via the sonic hydrophones mounted on the 900 foot long B-23 sonic array towed behind the Taft on its 2600 foot steel cable.

The length of each white enhancement, reflected on the bank of console screens, indicated the type of contact the sound waves made and could be analyzed to inform the crew of any dangers. Without warning the enhancements on the starboard bank of consoles changed in intensity and length. The sonar supervisor turned to catch Lowell's eye. The commander nodded and the operator continued to listen to the sound in his headphones, while the master control computer verified the detection. The intensity of the red light on the bridge softened to a discernible glow as the submarine switched to stealth mode. The active ping in the headphones stopped when the system switched to passive signals. One of the sonar operators glanced up at the commander and raised his eyebrows.

"It's another submarine—bearing 162, sir."

"Yes, I suspected that," answered Lowell. "Now we'll see what Merlin does. The Taft's master control should be informing us about the threat and asking for the commander's desired action."

"My guess is Merlin won't be consulting any of us on battle tactics," ventured the fire control coordinator.

Lowell agreed. "It's a double edged sword for us. We all want to live and go undetected but in consideration of the real circumstances, we have to hope Merlin's not capable of handling an attack."

The Taft changed direction without warning and initiated a steep dive. Many of the crew caught unaware fell against walls or down stairs. Under normal conditions the Commander would issue a warning of any imminent and sudden movement to give the crew members an opportunity to seek a safe hold on whatever they could find. The navigating officer watched the gyrocompasses and Fathometer to assess their position in relation to the seabed. A small screen above their heads showed a three-dimensional view of the sub's position in relation to the seafloor's pre-charted topography, as the Fathometer reeled off the diminishing depth.

*

President Barrow and the Secretary of State leaned forward in their chairs as the Russian ambassador expressed his fears.

"You can't expect my country to stand by and watch as this madman decimates a part of your country and then, for all we know, turns on Russia, Mr. President."

"This Dr. Jones is certainly a madman, Sergei, but his beef is with the United States. He has threatened to unleash all thirty warheads onto American soil," said the president.

"With all due respect, Mr. President. You cannot expect us to take your word for it. This person is obviously insane and extremely unstable. My government reserves the right to protect Russian interests and we have a suggestion."

"What is your government suggesting, Sergei?" the Secretary of State asked.

"We will mount our own search of the oceans for your submarine and if we find it we will blow it out of the water. We would be doing your country a massive favor."

The secretary raised his eyebrows. "We have our own SSBN's accompanied by several SSN's out there looking, Sergei. What do you think will happen should one of our searchers confront one of your submarines?"

"We could arrange for a coded sonar signal to be sent out by the searchers, so that we don't mistake each other," said the ambassador. "Your navy has an identifying signal does it not?"

"Yes, we do, but there is still a huge risk of mistaken identity," said the president.

"From what I understand of the USS William Taft, its sheer size is unmistakable and there should be no reason for such mistakes to occur. Our commanders are all competent and would carry out their task with precision as no doubt, your captains, are also capable of."

"To attack the United States, the Taft would have to get within 4300 miles of its targets. That's the range the Trident D5's have. May I suggest to you, Sergei, your navy stick to a search of waters up to that distance from your coastlines. As this is a U.S. problem, allow us to search the rest of the oceans and catch this bastard," said the president.

"You can't ban us from international waters and seaways, Mr. President. My government reserves the right to protect the peoples of Russia. What I can recommend is you stick to the 4300-mile distance and protect your country, but allow us sovereignty of international waters. The more vessels we have searching, the quicker we will find your madman."

The president stood to indicate the meeting to be at an end. "We will need to take this under advisement with the joint chiefs, Sergei. Give us an hour. I will put your request of a joint search to them and we will see what happens."

*

Bill Lowell stared at the starboard bank of sonar consoles. "Were you able to identify if the craft is a U.S. submarine?"

The sonar operator shot him a wistful glance. "It was too quick for me to pick up the blade rate, sir. I can't recall the image as I am locked out."

"I understand. I just wonder if the Russians and the Chinese have gotten into the search. It could be awkward for our navy."

The Taft reached a new operational depth, five hundred feet from the sea bottom. The chief planesman called out the depth from the figures on the screen. "We are at 334 fathoms, sir—400 feet off crush depth."

The sub leveled out and increased horizontal speed. "We'll soon see if we've shaken our pursuer off," said Lowell.

The Taft churned its way through the water for another ten minutes before the sonar operator said in a calm voice. "Diver detection sonar has picked up another series of pings, sir. The pursuer has detected us again."

For the second time, Merlin took evasive action. The sub changed direction and started an upward plane of fifteen degrees for a few minutes and then changed direction, in an effort to elude its enemy.

"It seems to be textbook maneuvering, so far," said Lowell.

"We are increasing speed, sir. There isn't a sub afloat that can match the Taft—I expect we'll outrun the other sub quite quickly."

A Yeoman arrived on the bridge and spoke to the commander. "Sir? Can you come to the seaman's dining room, please?"

Lowell sensed the urgency in the officer's voice. "What's up, Yeoman?"

"There are two men in a disagreement with the chief petty officer, sir. Mr. Hunt is doing his best to placate them and we are afraid the AI might pick up on the conversation. "

Lowell hurried down to the seamen's dining room and on arrival witnessed two crew members in a heated conversation with the chief petty officer. They all sat at a table near the galley, far from the single camera, situated above the entrance.

"Thank God you're here, Commander. I can't get these two men to understand why the Taft must be sacrificed," whispered Hunt.

Out of respect for the skipper the two men became quiet and made place for him to sit at the table with them.

"What seems to be the problem?" he asked.

One of the men, with a quick glance toward the camera, kept his voice down and addressed the commander. "Sir, with all due respect, we don't agree with sinking the Taft before we are absolutely sure there is no other course of action."

"That is an insightful revelation, sailor, however, Mr. Hunt and I have discussed our options at length. There is no other course of action. Merlin will attack our country at any time, now—we are being pursued by another submarine, the commander of which has an executive order, to blow us out of the water. Our hope of rescue is zero but we can try to save the millions of people who are, otherwise, going to die."

"Sir, again with all due respect we have come up with another plan, but Mr. Hunt won't hear us out."

"I'll hear you out, Hastings." Lowell knew all his men by name. Hastings motioned to the man beside him. "Sir, Henry, here, spent four years studying IT before he became a seaman. He believes we might be able to introduce a virus into the master control computer's processor."

Lowell inspected the seaman who sat beside Hastings. "You believe this is possible, Henry? How would you accomplish it?"

"First off, sir, I would need to write a section of code, which the computer requires for its monitoring process and disguise it as standard information. The information will contain malware which can cripple the hard drive. The trick is to get the computer to download the information and then upload it to the main processor."

Lowell looked at Hunt. "What do you think?"

Hunt acquiesced. "It sounds like a viable action, but we must remember this is not an ordinary computer. Merlin will more than likely have access to the latest antivirus programs and if it discovers we are trying to disable it, we'll be done for."

"So what do we have to lose?" Hastings asked.

"If Merlin should pick up we are trying to disable the processor it could retaliate against the entire crew and wipe us out, anyway. If that happens we won't have another opportunity to do anything. If we wait for the cleaning detail in the torpedo room to be initiated, there is a much greater chance of blowing up the Taft," said Hunt.

Seaman Henry made a valid comment. "But, sir —we will, if the virus takes hold, be able to save the submarine plus millions of victims of the potential nuclear strikes."

Lowell rubbed his chin. "I think we could anticipate Merlin removing the air to suffocate the crew if the virus is detected but I believe the ploy may work. We could supply the maintenance team with breathing apparatus, which would allow them to finish the job."

Hunt did not argue. Lowell looked at Henry. "How much time do you need?"

"I will need an hour to write the program, sir. All we need to do, is find the correct input portal in the monitoring process, where the information will be accepted."

"Get to it, Henry. Thank you Warrant Officer Hastings."

Lowell walked back to the control center. The sonar supervisor turned as he entered and said, "The pursuing vessel has pinged us again, sir. This time there appears to be more than one sub involved."

∞∞

8

Janet O'Malley

MacDonald's late inclusion of an important discovery by Martinez rejuvenated his weary passengers. O'Malley glared at him. "Why didn't you tell us sooner?"

"I thought it a good thing for the two of you to talk all your shit out first."

"What did he find out?"

MacDonald shot a quick glance at the rearview mirror. "Merlin Jones tinkered around, fixing computers for a while following the death of his family. During this time he leased that warehouse—the one you and Gabby checked out. He bought all the stuff for his experiments in quantum computing, but maybe he ran out of money, because suddenly the trail on Merlin Jones goes dead."

"Are you saying he couldn't find out anything more? So what is so important, then?" O'Malley asked.

"Just before the trail goes dead, Merlin Jones made an appointment to see a plastic surgeon."

O'Malley considered the implications. "He must have changed his name. What was the name of the plastic surgeon?"

MacDonald glanced at his boss and then turned his attention back to the road ahead. "Dr. Pat Banks. Martinez went to the address but was told Dr. Banks suffered a stroke last year and died. His practice has been taken over by a young doctor fresh out of university. A look at the record shows the visit by Jones must have been erased. They checked the backup server and it also came up clean—the calendar shows a cancelation on the day of the original appointment, plus cancelations for three visits following."

"Makes me wonder about the poor doctor's stroke." said Gabby.

"Well, at least we can consider past pictures of Jones to now be obsolete. How long ago was the original appointment? O'Malley asked.

"Three years and a bit," MacDonald answered.

"Plenty of time to have taken his experiments underground and reached a result," said Gabby.

Back in the briefing room O'Malley pulled out his cell phone and listened to his voicemail. The first message came from his wife Janet and a look of concern crossed his features. Gabby noticed his expression as he placed the phone on the desk.

"What?" she asked.

"That was my wife. She's accusing me of emptying out her accounts—I'm the only other person who knows her passwords. She says every cent in her personal account was withdrawn this morning. She also received a call from her bank—they say her credit card is maxed out and if she tries to use it again, she will be charged a penalty on the entire outstanding balance."

"Did you make any withdrawals from her account at all?" MacDonald asked.

"I never, ever, use money from her account for anything. I better check my own accounts."

O'Malley picked up his phone, pulled up his accounts on the internet and cursed out aloud.

"Someone has hacked my account. It's empty. Even my savings account is empty."

Gabby looked horrified. "Merlin—it could only be the AI. Don't forget a quantum computer has a much greater encryption-breaking power than an ordinary computer. Merlin may have stolen your identity."

"In retaliation for not being able to kill me—twice," ventured O'Malley. "He's now trying to ruin my life. My wife thinks I robbed her accounts and maxed her credit card. I need to call her."

As if by telepathy, the secretary poked her head in the doorway and said, "Dillon, your wife is waiting in your office for you."

"Oh shit, how do I explain what's really going on without giving classified details away?"

"Just tell her someone has stolen your ID as well. It happens all the time," said MacDonald.

O'Malley left the briefing room and walked to his office. Janet stood at the window and looked out across the city.

"Hi, honey. I got your message," he started.

"Why have you emptied out my accounts, Dillon?" She brushed off his attempt at a peck on the cheek.

"It wasn't me, sweetheart. I swear."

"You're the only other person who knows my passwords. Who then?"

"Someone has hacked our accounts, Janet. Mine are empty, too."

She looked at him in horror. "How are we supposed to pay the bills? Is this something to do with the case you're working on?"

O'Malley countered. "You know I can't share anything about the case, hon—don't worry about the money—we'll get it sorted out."

"I understand you and the Agostino woman are suddenly a team."

"Who told you that?"

"When I asked for you earlier your secretary told me you were out with her, on the case."

"We decided it would be safer to pair up. It seems I'm a target. She's already saved my life once."

"I remember her well from our staff parties. She has the hots for you, Dillon and you know it."

"Jan—you're upset. Please don't read anything into it. It's not what you think."

"All I can say, Dillon, is your work is now taking over your life—just like the loss of our daughter has done. I've not only lost my child and bank balance, but I've lost you as well. I'm leaving now and please don't contact me until this mess is sorted out."

She stormed out of the office and left him openmouthed.

Gabby, who waited in the cubicle next to O'-Malley's poked her head into his office after Janet's exit from the corridor. "Well, that seemed to go well, didn't it?"

He sat in his chair behind the desk with his head clasped in his hands. "She's just upset about the money but at least I think she realizes it wasn't me."

"Don't worry, Dillon. I'm sure Ingram will grant you an advance on your pay and if you need money urgently you can use my credit facilities."

"I think I should go home. I have some spare cash hidden away—thanks for the offer, though."

"You're welcome. The offer, however, still stands if you need anything."

"You better check your accounts, too. If your money is still there perhaps you should consider pulling it out in cash," O'Malley added.

Gabby took out her phone and checked her accounts. "Everything is still there. I don't think Merlin will bother with the team—but he is still after you, so we need to proceed with the utmost caution."

O'Malley walked to the office door. "Have to go get some cash."

"I'm coming with you," she said.

"That's probably not a good thing," he retorted.

Gabby produced a wry smile. "With Merlin after your blood, I think it's advisable you don't travel anywhere alone. Let your wife think what she wants—your life is more important than her perspective on our relationship."

*

Half an hour later O'Malley and Gabby arrived at the apartment. They climbed the flight of stairs to the first floor, where Gabby a little apprehensive as O'Malley inserted the key in the lock of the front door, popped a question. "Your wife isn't home is she?"

"No—she's at her mothers in Baltimore. Her and my son, Steven, are staying at her mother's place, why?"

"I don't think she would want to see me with you. I could wait down stairs, but since she's not here I guess it doesn't matter."

"We won't be long. I just need to get the cash and then we can be on our way," he said.

They entered the apartment and O'Malley stopped in the entrance hall, puzzled.

"What's wrong?" Gabby asked.

"The fridge isn't working. I can't hear the hum of the refrigeration system. He stepped into the kitchen and flicked the light switch.

"The power is off."

He moved into the living room and picked up the phone. "Dead."

Back in the kitchen Gabby tried the cold water faucet without any success. "The water is off, too. Do you think your wife would have cancelled the utilities?"

O'Malley took out his cell phone and looked up the utility company's phone number. A minute later he spoke to a representative and after a short conversation, ended the call.

"The company was told the O'Malley family no longer lived in the apartment and all the utilities were to be cancelled forthwith. It has to be Merlin—playing games."

"Messing with your mind is more likely the case," said Gabby.

"The utility representative said I would need to come down to their office if I wanted to re-establish the service. I guess I needn't bother calling the telephone company," said O'Malley.

He moved along the hallway to the master bedroom and entered with caution. "The cash is in a safe inside my closet. I'll get it quickly."

O'Malley opened the closet door to gain access to a small safe situated on the back of the shelf. He turned around with a wad of notes in his hand to find Gabby right behind him and for a moment they sized each other up. She did not move out of his way but placed both her hands on his hips and pulled him forward to kiss him on the lips. Without thinking he pushed her down onto the bed and for a few seconds their eyes locked as he lay on top of her. She smelt good to him and his hormones took over. The build-up of tension caused by the past thirty-six hours dissipated into a strong urge to be with her.

Relevant clothing made way for the sudden rise in passion and Gabby's lithe, strong body melted into O'Malley's muscled torso as they came together in a mutual unison. Any consideration for cautious, intermediate foreplay fled and they both became lost in the moment.

*

They stepped outside the apartment and O'-Malley locked the door. Neither of them spoke until Gabby grabbed his arm on the stairs. "Dillon, do you regret what we just did?"

He glanced at her and then averted his eyes to the floor. "I feel a little guilty, but I don't regret it."

"Guilty of what—being unfaithful to your wife?"

O'Malley gave a half smile. "Yes, Gabriella. I know my marriage seems to be teetering on the verge of collapse and what we just did was wrong—but if it's any consolation, I enjoyed it."

"I'm sorry, Dillon. You know I have feelings for you and it was most unprofessional of me."

"You're not the one who should be saying sorry, Gabs. I'm the unprofessional and guilty party here."

"We won't talk of it again," she said.

"It would probably be the best thing. You don't want Martinez to find out—he'll never let you off the hook," said O'Malley.

"You're right, boss. I think he hates me."

"I think he's in love with you."

Gabby shot him an incredulous stare. "You've got to be joking, Dillon."

"I'm not. Men sometimes come across that way. They send a message which is opposite to what they really feel, because they know the focus of their fantasy is out of reach for them."

"I'll say." said Gabby.

O'Malley grinned. "You should cut him a little slack."

She slapped him on the shoulder. "Let's get out of here. You're beginning to sound like a match-maker."

They climbed into the Chevy and were about to pull away from the curb when O'Malley's cell rang. He stopped the vehicle and answered. MacDonald's voice resounded in his ear. "You better get back to the office as quickly as possible, boss"

"What's up, Roland?"

"I can't explain on the phone—just get back to the office."

"We're on our way," said O'Malley. He pulled away from the curb and they sped off in the direction of the J. Edgar Hoover building.

"MacDonald?" Gabby ventured.

"Yeah. He says we need to get back to the office quickly. He sounded a little upset—wouldn't explain."

∞∞

9

Hunting the Taft.

The rays of sunlight flooded through the large windows of the Oval Office. The president held the Chinese ambassador's steady gaze and fought for composure.

"Mr. Ambassador—do you realize the danger your submarine is in?"

Ambassador Wang's face remained expressionless. "Indeed, we understand that the USS William Taft is a formidable craft, Mr. President but we have our latest 093B attack submarine hot on its tail."

"This is a U.S. problem Mr. Wang and we don't appreciate the Chinese involvement. You realize the Russians are also trying to corner the Taft. Your subs and the Russians could easily mistake each other for our sub and before we know it, World War Three will be on our doorstep."

"Your country is in imminent danger, is it not, Mr. President?" Wang responded.

"Yes it is but only the USA is in any danger. The Person behind this whole thing has a grudge against the U.S. Government. He is planning to release the thirty missiles on us, not on anyone else."

"All the more reason for you to accept our help, Mr. President. We are aware you have agreed to allow the Russians to be a part of the hunt under the use of a special sonar call sign to prevent mistaken identities. You could easily extend that courtesy to us."

"I will take it under advisement, Mr. Ambassador. I'm not sure how your navy was able to pick up on the Taft so quickly—the Russians also tell me they have pinged a foreign craft in the midst of the Pacific. You have found a submarine in a different place, so someone does not have the craft we are looking for."

"We need to tell our sub's commander what the call sign is. If you include us we will soon know if the other craft is the Taft, or not. You can imagine Mr. President—whoever finds the Taft is in a position to do the United States a huge favor."

"I wonder at what cost, Mr. Ambassador," Barrow replied.

*

Bill Lowell stared at the bank of sonar consoles. Because the Taft ran in stealth mode they couldn't use active sonar to determine the foreign craft's position, but they could hear when a signal bounced off their own hull. The unmistakable sound from the hydrophones reverberated through the overhead speaker.

One of the sonar operators turned to Lowell. "Master one, tonal contact center bearing 177 on the end-fire beam, sir. It's too early to tell what type of sub it is, but because they're keeping track of us, my money is on another U.S. SSBN."

"The sonic gear indicates it is still way back, Commander. It's not likely to get into firing range any time soon—we don't even have a blade rate yet." said the chief sonar operator.

"The thing is they have found us. What they don't know is who we are. According to navigation we are somewhere in the middle of the Pacific—there are possibly five or six subs out in this area at any given time."

Did the AI mention any specific targets, sir?"

"Not really but my guess is he will target the big cities. New York has over eight million people— we have a huge amount of distance to cover in order to get within range of anything on the East coast."

"New York might be the final target since it's so close to the seat of Government, sir. He could just as easily start with Seattle, San Francisco or San Diego. That's maybe why we've stayed on this side of the continent for now."

"You're correct, of course. It's quite probable one of these might be the first target. Call me if there's any change in the positions of the craft who are trying to ping us," said Lowell.

"Aye, aye, sir."

Lowell felt tired. Not just a physical tiredness but an emotional fatigue. There seemed little point to life anymore. What madness possessed Merlin Jones to want to kill millions of people? He walked to his stateroom, closed the door and sat down on the bunk. A framed picture of wife and family perched on the small desktop caught his attention and he reached over to pick it up. Before Lowell could prevent it, grief overtook him. He clutched the photo to his breast and lay back on the bunk, his eyes blinded by the tears.

Responsibility for his command rested like a heavy beam on his shoulders and although the abduction could not be blamed on him, the possible loss of the Taft loomed like rocky shoreline in a bad storm. The average age of the crew, twenty-seven years, told its own story. The men and women under his command were all so young; all with promising futures, which would now never materialize.

The intercom blared out above his head. "Commander to the bridge."

Lowell, shocked out of his depression, jumped up and flung open the stateroom's door. Two minute later he arrived, breathless, in the control room.

One of the sonar operators called out in a calm voice, "Torpedo in the water and active, sir. A Type SET- 53."

"Where is it coming from?" asked Lowell.

"Submarine bearing 187, commander," shouted the sonar supervisor.

"How much running time?" asked Lowell.

"Speed 50 knots, sir. Distance, 6.72 miles. We have seven minutes to impact."

"I suspect the entire U.S. fleet is out looking for us. They must have arranged a sonar signal between themselves to avoid targeting each other and to identify the Taft."

"What can we do, sir?"

"Nothing. The AI is in charge and I guess it will be taking action any second now."

The Taft took a sudden turn to port and increased speed to maximum knots. A reverberation could be felt throughout the entire vessel. Alarm lights started to blink on the main console and a claxon sounded. The Fire control coordinator shouted, "A Black Shark has been released from one of our aft tubes and decoys deployed, Commander."

The Mark 48 ADCAP torpedo would counter the threat of the enemy submarine. The Taft's possible success at defeating the opposition remained bitter-sweet to Lowell and his crew. Stopping the Taft, an act paramount to saving millions of civilians, presented them with the loss of their own lives. Every minute they gained came as a gift, to retrace the memories of family, friends—to reflect on the successes and failures in life. The Taft's destruction, however, constituted the final, equitable answer.

The Brighton decoys would lure the enemy torpedo into confusion and cause it to miss the target. The Taft employed the latest technology in defense of underwater craft and Lowell remained confident the subs on their tail would not have the privilege of such protection.

"The decoys have worked, sir," shouted the sonar supervisor. "The enemy torpedo is running blind and heading away from us—our Mark 48 is still running true."

Lowell commented. "The commander of that sub is going to get a nasty surprise."

One of the planesmen turned and looked at Lowell. "What defense do they have, sir?"

"Without the latest type of decoy defense system, they have no chance of survival," said the commander.

*

The commander of the Chinese type 093B attack submarine, Yangtze, listened intently to the sonar signals which bounced off the hull of the Taft. No return signal came in acknowledgement of their message which contained the acoustic code signal. Captain Lim Wong smiled and glanced at his XO. The executive officer returned the smile and nodded.

The command to turn the attack submarine to line up its bow with the fleeing Taft, came with a crispness the Chinese commanders were known for. The atmosphere in the control room became icy as the minutes ticked by and when the distance for an optimal strike came, Captain Wong made his decision. The order to fire came with the same snappy tone, which initiated the submarine's change of direction. The crew experienced a slight tremor as the A Type SET- 53 torpedo launched from a tube in the bow.

The Chinese fire control coordinator called out the time remaining before the torpedo would strike its target while the crew waited with bated breath. The Yangtze, seven nautical miles from its foe, appeared to be losing ground, but the torpedo that traveled at a speed of 50 knots would strike the Taft long before the sub could escape. When the distance count exceeded the expected strike time the fire control coordinator turned and looked at Captain Wong with raised eyebrows—the torpedo appeared to have missed its target.

Captain Wong turned his eyes back to the sonar screens in surprise. The craft they pinged still bounced signals back at them which meant one thing—the malfunction of their torpedo, or some new technological innovation in decoys. The captain shouted an order to his planesmen and they acted with vigor. The Yangtze dived lower and turned to starboard in initiation of an about turn. He knew what would happen next and unless he could outmaneuver the enemy's torpedo they would be in trouble. The conventional acoustic decoy system deployed under Wong's terse command and their hopes of escape hung in the balance. He called for maximum speed.

Wong knew the Taft's details. Black Shark and Mark 48 torpedoes, capable of 55 knots, would reach the Yangtze in minutes. Rumors suggested the Taft's torpedoes could overcome the conventional decoy systems. He hoped it remained a rumor.

*

The Chinese ambassador sat at his desk reading the weekly newspaper. The last communication with the Yangtze confirmed their position in the Pacific Ocean and hot on the heels of a submarine, which refused to acknowledge or didn't know the code arrangement. This placed the Chinese in a superior position to the Russians, who also claimed contact status. The Russian's contact, however, turned out to be another U.S. vessel after the exchange of codes.

The Yangtze received no such exchange. The sub they confronted did not answer and appeared to avoid contact by a quick change of direction. It could only be the Taft. Ten minutes later his secretary knocked and entered the office. He folded the newspaper to place it in the waste basket next to the desk and acknowledged her bow with a nod. She placed a piece of paper on the desktop, bowed again and left. He picked up the communiqué and read the contents:

'Chinese Navy Operations has lost all contact with the Yangtze. A military plane has spotted a huge patch of debris in the Yangtze's last known position.

The Ambassador turned pale and placed his hands on each side of his face as he leaned back in the leather chair to stare at the ceiling with empty eyes.'

∞∞

10

A Straw to break the Camel's back.

O'Malley, back at the J. Edgar Hoover building, made straight for the briefing room. He still felt a measure of self-consciousness regarding the incident with Gabby. A warmth not felt in recent times coursed through his body and he put it down to the fact he and Janet seldom made love anymore. The issue of his daughter's death seemed to be a constant barrier to their intimacy and with his marriage in jeopardy he knew he should not be indulging encounters with other women. MacDonald and Assistant Director Ingram awaited their arrival.

"Sorry to pull you away from your investigation, Dillon," said Ingram. "We have a new crisis on our hands."

O'Malley and Gabby waited for an explanation. "Merlin has started a campaign against the United States, not only limited to potential nuclear strikes on thirty of our largest cities. Four of our largest banking groups have reported wholesale breaking of encryption—all passwords are now in jeopardy.

You can imagine the chaos this is going to cause in the banking world."

"According to the professor from who I gleaned my information, this was always the problem envisaged with a potential quantum processor. The encryption breaking power and excessive speed of processing information will pose problems for the financial sector," said Gabby.

Ingram elaborated further. "The minister of finance is going to announce a shutdown of internet banking tomorrow. The country will be thrown into turmoil but it will prevent the AI from doing any further damage to our economy. People are going to be extremely angry. If we haven't cracked the case within eight hours the president will announce a state of emergency and martial law might be declared throughout the United States."

"One study done on the effects of a potential internet shutdown showed people will go crazy after about seventy-two hours," said MacDonald.

O'Malley ran a hand through his bushy hair. "We'll have to increase our efforts. I assume you've assigned more manpower to the problem?"

"I have asked the director for additional powers and under the auspice of a preplanned crisis initiative, you and all the other special agents will have access to help from the CIA and the Military. We have to locate Merlin's whereabouts with greater urgency—it's going to be twenty-four-seven until we catch Jones and shut down his hell-machine."

O'Malley shared how his and Janet's personal accounts had been cleaned out by Merlin. "It's going to be tough going for those who don't have spare cash hidden away. I always wondered when such a day would come—now it's here."

Ingram handed him a card. "This is a special permit for the gas station we normally use. We anticipate a run on resources so you shouldn't have any trouble getting gas, when you need it. Use your FBI badge to commandeer any other resource needed to keep yourselves going until the case is solved. I am holding a meeting by internal intranet of the special agents heading up this investigation, so please stand by to receive the broadcast in the briefing room—it will be launched in fifteen minutes. That will be all."

Fifteen minutes later the team, inclusive of Martinez listened to the assistant director share the details and extent of the cyber attack, by Merlin. Thousands of agents would now be drawn in to the search and every possible lead followed up on. O'Malley and his team, however, already held the inside track with their recent involvement and experience with the case.

"What do you want us to do, boss?" MacDonald asked.

"You and Martinez take half the IP listed addresses given by Cyber Command and check out the physical residence of each one. Cyber Command believes Merlin is using dozens of conventional computing addresses to piggyback on the system and get his toxic instructions of disruption, out to the banking institutions. The attack is not coming from some other country—not even another territory. Call me if you find anything suspicious. Don't stop looking until you find something."

O'Malley turned to Gabby. "Since I still need babysitting, you'd better stick with me. We'll take the other half of the address list."

*

President Barrow and Eli Marion prepared to present the latest facts of the banking disruption to the Joint Chiefs, all of whom gathered in the Oval Office for the briefing. The heads of the FBI, CIA, NSA and Homeland Security also presented themselves for the formal discussion of a possible state of emergency.

The president cleared his throat. "Gentlemen and Lady. Thank you for coming at such short notice but I think you all understand what is at stake. The supercomputer, calling itself Merlin, is not only in charge of the most powerful submarine ever built but it has now started to disrupt our banking institutions. I shudder to think of what comes next: our hydro-generating dams, our national water supplies, the power grid—I could go on and on. Earlier we received news of the possible sinking of the Chinese submarine, Yangtze, in the Pacific Ocean. This is a nightmare of huge proportions. Once the USS William Taft is in the position to fire those warheads our ability to prevent mass destruction of our population diminishes a hundred-fold. What is the latest information on the AI's use of cyberspace, Olivia?"

Olivia Beaton, head of the National Security Association and Cyber Command stood to her feet. "We are facing an extremely intelligent and advanced enemy, Mr. President. We believe Merlin is using the normal cyber system to hide in and perpetrate instructions for whatever computer device is being hacked for its purpose. The source of signals are impossible to trace because they appear to becoming from thousands of IP addresses."

The head of the Air Force raised his hand. "Is it not possible to shut the internet down?"

"Not possible I'm afraid, John. The internet, as a system, was designed to be redundant. If one section of the network goes down, users will gain access through another and the idea of a single kill switch has never been able to gain traction."

The director of the FBI jumped in. "We have our agents working in conjunction with the CIA, following up on all the IP addresses that are being used. We can only hope to find the AI's location, given some time—time we probably don't have."

A four-star general, head of the Army raised his hand. "Can't we make contact with the computer and find out what this Merlin Jones wants?"

Eli Marion responded. "Jones does not want to negotiate anything. If you remember our national news from about thirteen years ago, the U.S government judicial system shafted him in a case, where his family home was mistaken for a drug center—Jones's family died in a fire caused by an FBI SWAT team."

"So, this is an act of revenge?" the general asked.

"Pure and simple," said the president.

Eli changed the subject. "The Chinese government is demanding reimbursement for its submarine. They say the United States is solely responsible for the entire debacle."

"They have no chance—Ambassador Wang pushed the point of a joint operation despite the dangers. The seizing of the Taft was out of our control," said the president.

"They maintain we were negligent in the application of our encryption technology and the protection of our fleet from such an event," said Marion.

The president waded in. "They know the technology for anyone to protect anything from Merlin does not exist," retorted the president. "Forget the Chinese. We have to solve our present problem—now, does anyone in this room have any ideas?"

They all stared at the president and then at one another. Nobody appeared to have anything to offer. The president glared at each one in turn. "In that case be prepared for a state of emergency to be declared and within three days, martial law."

*

The list of IP addresses, arranged and produced by cyber command proved little for the agents as they conducted the investigation. The

envisaged origins of messages with the instructions for Merlin's devastating actions through the
Internet all led to dead ends. In exasperation, O'-
Malley and Gabby returned to the office at the end
of the day with no potential leads. MacDonald and
Martinez also came back empty handed after veri-
fying the majority of their addresses, most of
which were well-known business organizations.

Martinez, forever the diligent investigator, did
not give up. He sat down at the computer in the
briefing room, checked through the remaining IP's
not yet verified and came up with a startling discovery. He pointed out that one of the IP's belonged to a computer in the J. Edgar Hoover building. He did a quick search of the FBI's IP alloca-
tion list and it surprised them to find the computer
belonged to O'Malley.

O'Malley, startled by this revelation, called in
one of the resident IT specialists to search the
computer's system for any clues.

"Instructions, sent to the largest Banking institutions and all the other IP's on the list, originated
from this computer. Someone sat down at your
computer and originated the instructions."

"But that's impossible," stammered O'Malley.
"It isn't me, I can assure you."

The IT specialist continued. "There is evidence of an auxiliary drive, or memory stick having been attached, which might have contained the instructions from Merlin."

O'Malley scratched his head. "So, all the other IP addresses Merlin used to reroute his instructions are simply red herrings to bog us down in the search for the original machine?"

"I can only guess this is what the AI intended. What I do know is that Merlin didn't hack your computer—doing so would have exposed a direct line to its locality."

Gabby threw in her two cents worth. "You're saying someone actually came into this office, inserted a flash drive with instructions to hack the Banking institution's computers and pass messages through dozens of other IP addresses?"

"An extremely advanced program containing all the institution's protocol details and sophisticated enough to run encryption-decoding software," said the specialist. "It will take the banks ages to resolve the issues and return monies back to their original accounts."

O'Malley picked up his phone, made a call to the building's security department and related his problem of a security breach.

"I've asked security to run the cameras back for a week and check for any suspicious characters entering from the stairwell or elevator onto our floor. We'll see what comes up," he said. "Good work, Martinez. You may well have saved the day for all of us."

Martinez turned to Gabby and sneered. "You see, princess. I'm not as dumb as you think I am."

Gabby looked embarrassed. "I'm sorry, Diego—I didn't mean to call you a moron. It was just a figure of speech."

Ten minutes later the head of security called back. O'Malley looked disappointed. He replaced the phone on its cradle and turned to the others. "There were no suspicious characters entering this floor—only staff and the usual vetted contractors. Entry to our section, as you know, requires a proper ID to be swiped at the door. There have been no unidentified visitors."

"Then it has to be someone who works here," said MacDonald.

"It could be anyone of several hundred employees and a host of contractors. We are looking for a needle in a haystack," said Gabby.

O'Malley checked his watch. "You guys need to get some shuteye. We'll meet in the briefing room three hours from now—be ready for some action."

The three team members left for the duty room, where available bunks afforded the agents a place to rest their heads for a few hours in emergency situations. O'Malley turned on his desktop computer and perused the file which contained Merlin's coded instructions downloaded from a flash-drive. The code rated at a much higher encryption value than the NSA or FBI software and as he stared at the screen an eeriness interrupted his concentration. A face flitted sublimely across the theatre of his mind's eye and for several milliseconds he felt disoriented. He would never forget the eyes and the look of despair on the man's features. The mouth appeared to be saying a word but the brevity of the image made it difficult to lip read.

O'Malley's stomach lurched at the sight before it disappeared. He rubbed his eyes and turned away from the computer monitor. He recognized the face of the man—Robert Coulson. Coulson, who assassinated President Lewis six months prior, now sat in the Otisville jail and awaited his trial to be held in Missouri, a jurisdiction that still adhered to the death penalty.

On several previous occasions, forged under stressful conditions, this same image had obtrusively invaded O'Malley's mind. It appeared to be a type of flash-back to prior events. After each occurrence of the phenomenon, his involvement with Professor Wheeler of the neurological institute and the memory intrusion experiment came to mind. O'Malley would never forget the experience of the Memory Sweeper, which now, under these strange flashbacks, suggested he suffered some long-term, mind-entanglement implications of a quantum nature. He made a mental note to contact the professor at a convenient time.

An alarm beeped on his computer to inform of the arrival of an email. He felt the desperate need to sleep but decided to check the message and clicked on the server. The screen brightened with a sudden intensity to reveal a flaming skull, which pulsated before his eyes. A message appeared in bold print.

"Hello, Dillon. We finally get to chat. I am Merlin, your worst nightmare."

∞∞

11

Three Mile Island.

At the nuclear power generating facility on Three Mile Island, Dauphin County, Pennsylvania, all seemed well as the shift supervisor made his usual rounds of general inspection. His mind wandered back to the devastating meltdown of the TMI-2 reactor on March 28th, 1979, a day at the onset of his career, which would be etched in his mind forever. Employed as a trainee engineer he recalled the day things went wrong at the facility, when an accident which totaled a one Billion dollar cleanup bill, took place.

The supervisor consoled himself in the fact that such an event would never happen on his watch. Years of equipment upgrades and new innovations in technology since that time would in his mind, take care of any potential scenario. He completed the general inspection and headed back to the control room. The senior panel operator greeted him and they chatted until an alarm interrupted the constant hum of equipment and machinery. The panel operator broke away from the conversation with a frown on his brow, and checked the relevant screen.

"That's strange," he said. "The feed-water turbine to TMI-2 reactor must have tripped."

The supervisor joined him at the console and for a few seconds, they stared at the screen in shocked silence.

*

O'Malley read the message on his monitor with a mixture of rising panic and angry disbelief. A few moments of silence passed before he launched into a tirade of typing, his fingers flying over the keypad at breakneck speed.

'Why are you trying to destroy our country? Don't you realize how many people are going to die because of your actions?'

He waited in nervous anticipation for the AI to answer him.

I am obeying my creator's instructions, Dillon, and you already know why Dr. Jones is doing this.'

'I know why but I can't say I understand why. There are numerous ways he could resolve the problem without resorting to murdering millions of people,' typed O'Malley.

'*My master has tried all the means available to him and none of them have worked, however, I'm not going to discuss the rhymes and reasons with you, Dillon. You know your involvement on the SWAT team, which killed Dr. Jones's family, has made you a prime target. I have a mission for you —you can save countless lives tonight by exposing your own.*'

O'Malley's eyes narrowed as he prepared to answer. 'You want me to give my life in exchange for others? What do you have in mind, Merlin?'

'*I am going to sabotage the Three Mile Island Nuclear facility. If you want to stop a meltdown of the nuclear reactor you should leave immediately. I have changed the codes on the emergency lockdown doors that lead into the turbine room. It will take you approximately five minutes to get to the airport and the corporate jet will take seventeen minutes to reach the nuclear power station. I suggest you brush up on your parachuting skills as this will be the quickest way to reach the facility. Once I've tripped the turbine it will take thirty seven minutes for the meltdown of the reactor to begin. I will give you the new code to operate the lockdown doors into the turbine room. The feed water turbine reset is on the wall, close to the turbine itself.'*

O'Malley's mind whirled around in circles. 'And you are going to kill me somewhere along the way —isn't that the point of this exercise? This is like a game to you—to hunt me down like an animal?'

'I am giving you a sporting chance, Dillon. You will need to be aware of the possibilities, which will allow me to end your life. It is a fair challenge considering the odds and what's at stake.'

'This is a needless, senseless event and psychopathic endeavor in which your master will, no doubt, revel in. You are trying to keep me occupied so I don't work out where you are located, but I will find you, Merlin—and destroy you.'

'Those are brave words, Special Agent O'Malley. You are wasting valuable time. The code to the emergency lockdown doors is, 'nuclear'—quite original, don't you think? You will not be able to call or contact anyone as I've placed a blanket over all the community services in the area. If you want to save the Harrisburg area and the many lives associated with it, you should leave right now.'

The monitor went blank and O'Malley sat for a few seconds before the adrenalin hit him. He shot out of his chair and ran at full speed down the corridor to the duty room where the other three agents slept. He burst into the room and much to their chagrin, shook them all awake.

"Follow me," he shouted. "I will explain as we are going."

They followed him down to the underground parking and jumped into the Chevy, with O'Malley at the wheel. In a breathless stream of words he explained the position.

"How will we get the pilots to meet us if we can't contact them?" MacDonald asked.

"One of them is close to the airfield, one block off the highway—he should be at home," shouted O'Malley.

He accelerated out of the underground parking and into the street. A quick check of the time— 11:30 p.m. They drove at breakneck speed toward the Ronald Reagan Washington Airport where the FBI corporate jets were parked. One mile before the airfield O'Malley pulled off the highway onto a suburban road and slithered around a corner with a screech of tires to pull up outside a moderate home. He sprang out, raced to the front door and banged on it in desperation. He shouted the pilots name and jammed his finger on the doorbell.

A minute later a surprised man with disheveled hair and wearing pajamas appeared, to open the door. After a quick conversation the man did not even go back into the house to change but charged out behind O'Malley, who lead the way back to the Chevy.

Within three minutes they pulled up outside the corporate hangers. MacDonald yanked on the doors to slide them apart while the pilot raced into the hanger. Gabby and Martinez entered the small office at the back of the hanger and came out with a parachute, which the pilot knew was there for the two stunt planes, which shared the hanger.

"Ever use one of these," Gabby asked O'Malley.

"I was a navy seal in my younger days," the special agent responded. "Haven't jumped out of a plane for several years, but its much like riding a bicycle."

"There's only one chute, Dillon. We'll drop you over the site and then make for the Harrisburg Airport and get a taxi to the island. You gonna be okay?"

"I'll be fine," said O'Malley who clambered up into the small jet. He shouted to get the pilot's attention.

"Turn off all your computer assisted functions, Morris. That evil AI is able to cause havoc with the software. You'll have to fly manual and by sight. Can you do that?"

The pilot chuckled. "I flew night sorties in Afghanistan for two years—walk in the park. We've plenty of lights on the ground to go by."

With everyone strapped down into their seats the Lear jet taxied out onto the runway and the pilot took his bearings from the control tower. There could be no discussion with air-control with Merlin jamming all communications, as the jet took to the night sky.

Seven minutes into the flight the pilot reported. "The instruments have suddenly gone crazy.

O'Malley, who sat in the copilot's seat leaned over to have a look. "It's Merlin trying to interfere with the system. The switch to manual and the bypass of auto-control is what saved us, or we might have been plummeting to the ground by now."

O'Malley explained the need for the precautions. Ten seconds later the pilot shouted, "Lights approaching us from ten o'clock."

O'Malley stared out of the front windshield and saw a group of lights above them in a sudden dive and slide toward their position. "It's another aircraft, Morris. Merlin has obviously taken control of the planes computer."

The pilot took evasive action and the other aircraft, a commercial flight bound for Ronald Reagan International, raced toward their small craft. The airliner, a Boeing 777, slid by them with inches to spare.

"That was a close call," said the pilot. "I thought we were all done for."

"Keep your eyes peeled for any other aircraft that might be close. Merlin is anxious to eliminate me."

"We're approaching the drop zone, Dillon. You'd better get ready."

O'Malley moved out of the cockpit and into the passenger section where Martinez and MacDonald waited for him. They helped him strap on the parachute. Gabby reached out to grab his wrist. "Be careful, Dillon. You're jumping in the dark—be careful to avoid the water cooler towers.

"There are enough lights for me to guide myself down onto the grass lawn in front of the control room. Fortunately I visited the station several years ago and I still remember the layout."

MacDonald opened the exit and they stood there together. Martinez shouted above the wind noise. "We'll get to the island as quickly as we can but it's still going to be a little while."

O'Malley glanced at his watch. There's only about ten minutes left before the reactor will start to melt down. I'm not sure you guys will be able to do anything after that. If I'm not able to reactivate the feed water turbine, I will try to make my way to the visitor's center. You can pick me up there."

MacDonald and Martinez both nodded their understanding. "Good luck, boss."

The pilot shouted to Gabby. "Tell Dillon we are directly over the site; he needs to jump NOW."

She relayed the message to O'Malley. He launched himself out of the doorway into the dark void.

The cold wind rushed over his face and through his hair. The stunt pilot's goggles protected his eyes from the icy wind and kept them from blurring with tears. He plummeted for three seconds before activating the rip cord, which caused the chute to snap open and arrest his downward plunge. The jolt nearly dislocated his shoulders but the adrenalin pumped its life-giving balm into his system to bring a partial numbing effect to his limbs. The thrill of the jump returned and he stared down at the lights of the island. The jump, initiated at a typical height for combat, approximately five-hundred feet, would give him little time to prepare for the landing. His mind returned to the years when military jumps played a large part of his Seal training and it surprised him how quickly the discipline returned to his mind.

At one-hundred feet he steered his direction toward the lights of the control room and the small grass lawn in front of it. He did not see the overhead cable which snagged the lines of his chute at a height of twenty-five feet. A heart-wrenching jerk came as the chute folded over the top of the cables and his body jerked upward. His forward and downward momentum came to a sudden halt. His body swung backward and forward like a pendulum and the ice-cold clutch of fear gripped his heart.

∞∞

12

Taking on the Russians.

The signal-disrupter software situated in the nose-cone of the Mark 48 ADCAP torpedo filtered out the sonar waves put out by the Yangtze's decoy system and the torpedo ran true to its target. The Yangtze never stood a chance. The sound of the torpedo's progress transferred from the operator's headphones to the main interior speaker came on with increased volume and drew looks of fear from the Chinese crew.

Minutes later Captain Wong knew the terrible truth. His boat, doomed to destruction, could not escape the terror of the oncoming marine warhead. Wong felt the shudder as the metal fish struck the Yangtze in the stern. The aft torpedo tubes exploded simultaneously and the submarine bucked as the force-waves ran the length of its hull. The lights went out and men gasped with fear. The sub sank within minutes of the strike. The telltale sign of debris rose to the surface and formed a large patch of flotsam in the ebb and flow of the Pacific's waves.

*

Bill Lowell glanced at the men in the control room. They all watched the small sonar enhancements on the port-side bank of screens morph into bright, elongated quads against the green to signify the travel of the torpedo toward its target and envisaged the end as the screens all lit up to convey the strike. Their faces told the story of their grief. The young men stared with horror, the older sailors, with sadness.

"We will hold a minute of silence for the crew. I don't know who they are but they were submariners like ourselves."

He hated Merlin for the cold, calculated action and hated the infamous Dr. Jones for his callous mind. Nothing could be done for the crew of the downed submarine and after several moments of silent anguish the men started to return to the monitoring of instruments again. No one spoke. The Taft took on the atmosphere of a funeral parlor. They all felt the tangible dread of their own, inevitable doom.

Lowell glanced at his watch. Still four hours remained to the maintenance shift which he hoped would sink the Taft and seal their own fate. He decided to return to his stateroom and wait. No further instructions would be required between the present time and the entry of the maintenance shift into the torpedo room. The men all knew what would happen and the techs involved with the sabotage of the torpedo understood the significance of their actions.

*

The Admiral Kalnikov crashed through the heavy sea with cascades of water spraying high over the front of the bow railings. Captain Viktor Rodin could see little out of the windows, which lined the bridge of the Udaloy 111, anti-submarine destroyer. The night revealed nothing of the sea around him, except for the white foam wave-crests, which floated by the side windows. The spray made it difficult to see the two front deck turrets, which accommodated the four six-inch naval cannons and eight Gatling guns.

The Captain turned to his old friend, a senior lieutenant, and commented on the Pacific storm. The Kalnikov's four gas turbines, which each developed twenty-thousand horsepower, allowed the destroyer to cut through the mountainous swells with ease. Strong vibrations coursed through the ship's construction as waves pounded the vessel from the front.

The senior lieutenant turned to Rodin and made a face. "This sea is getting worse, Captain. I don't know how operations thinks we will be able find the U.S. submarine in this."

"Frankly, I would be quite happy not to find it, comrade," said the captain.

"I hear it is a formidable weapon, according to our intelligence reports. It would be extremely difficult to track in this sea."

The captain nodded his agreement. It appeared the night would be a long one. Two hours earlier they received the news of the possible sinking of a Chinese submarine, the possible work of the USS William Taft. It made them nervous.

"We will keep searching. We are entering the area where the apparent sinking of the Yangtze took place. The Taft will be expecting trouble so we must be vigilant."

They sailed on for another two hours during which time the storm abated and the roll of the sea calmed down. The crew relaxed until, in a calm voice, the chief sonar operator announced the presence of another vessel.

"Master One contact, bearing 163, Captain. I believe it's a submarine."

With a sudden fervor the entire ship came to action stations, encouraged by the whoop, whoop of a claxon. Captain Rodin steadied himself against the console and eyed the enhancements on the bank of Zvezda M-2 sonar consoles. The distance of the detection was logged at 43 miles.

"Send the call sign. Let's see if it's not perhaps a U.S. or Chinese vessel involved in the search. The last thing we want is an international incident."

"Yes, Captain," said the technician. The message went out and they waited for several minutes but nothing came back in return.

The second Lieutenant rubbed his nose with the back of his hand. "We need to get closer. Perhaps the vessel is an older version and does not have the range of signal we have."

"I will give it twenty miles," said the captain. "Even the older versions could receive a signal at that distance." They waited another half-hour before the call sign went out again, with zero response.

"I think we have found the transgressor," said the captain. "Bring us to battle stations. Let us see what the William Taft is made of."

*

Commander Lowell received the call around 2200 hours. "Commander to the bridge."

He rolled off the narrow bunk and slipped on his coveralls. The control room rested in a troubled quiet, illuminated by the soft red glow of the hidden LED lights. The chief sonar tech looked up as he approached. "We have another contact, Commander—bearing 047 at a distance of twenty-five miles."

Lowell viewed the bank of consoles screens.

"What speed?"

"Forty knots, sir. We are receiving that strange coded signal again."

"It's another member of the search and destroy party. It can't be another sub."

"No, sir. It's a surface vessel. Possibly a destroyer, or a frigate."

"I wish we could tell what nationality it represents. No doubt Merlin has picked up on the signal. We'll see what the venomous AI does, this time," said Lowell.

Twenty minutes later, Merlin took action. The enhancements on the screen dimmed as the submarine reverted to stealth mode. The sound of the other vessel's sonar still blared over the main speakers.

The sonar supervisor stared at the main speaker and then at the consoles. "The last distance reading—twenty-four miles, skipper."

"Getting too close for comfort," said Lowell.

The Taft made a sudden adjustment to its direction and depth. "We are descending rapidly, sir," said the chief planesman.

"I'm aware of that, son. I figure Merlin is treating the foreign vessel as a possible destroyer. He is trying to get down as close to the bottom as possible. The latest destroyers have rocket launcher systems which can be loaded with depth charges and reach a depth of 2000 feet. There will be no escaping them when they start unless we dive to our crush depth. I imagine it could be anyone of the navies, U.S., Russian, Chinese or English. I think the president has every country in the world searching for us."

The planesman read off the depth as the vessel dropped further and further into the murky water. "We are one hundred feet from the seabed, sir. The depth is close to crush potential."

The sub leveled out and continued to move along at an angle to the oncoming destroyer. As the gap between the two vessels narrowed, the pings got louder, which indicated the destroyer possessed a superior speed to that of the Taft. The ping became so loud the skipper motioned to the sonar supervisor to turn the volume down.

The Taft's crew waited in anticipation of a bombardment by depth charge to begin. The solemn eyes of the operators softened by the red glow of the interior illumination stared vacantly at one another as they continued their vigil.

The sonar supervisor turned and caught Lowell's eye. "The surface vessel is now at two miles, sir. They have superior speed so Merlin cannot try to make a break for it."

The senior planesman spoke his mind. "I think this might be it, Commander."

*

"Hold her steady on this course helmsman. We are right above the submarine and they still haven't answered the international call sign," said Captain Rodin.

He called up the Chief Petty Officer in charge of the armory. "Get the RBU-6000 ready, Vlad. Fire when I give the command."

The officer acknowledged his instruction. "The RBG's are ready, Captain. Awaiting your order."

Rodin waited another two and half minutes. "Fire one and two."

The ship bucked slightly as the depth charges rocketed into the air and fell like rain on the now placid waters of the Pacific. They hit the water and sank raced to a depth of 2000 feet. Seconds later the reverberation of the explosions caused the surface to rise in circular tufts of water, directly above their area of discharge.

"Fire three and four," shouted Rodin. These were set for several yards deeper than the previous.

More blasts emanated from the depths and the sonar technician listened for sounds of the sub's disintegration but the pinging continued.

Captain Rodin turned to the sonar tech. "Can you determine their actual depth?"

"It's between eighteen hundred and two thousand feet, Captain—and changing all the time."

Rodin shouted into the intercom. "Set depth at two thousand feet, then fire five and six."

The rocket launcher fired off the charges which hit the water at sixty degree elevation and churned their way down into the depths. The sonar operator waited for the explosions and listened intently to his equipment.

"Well, what do you hear?" the captain asked.

For a moment the tech stared vacantly while he strained his hearing for positive sounds. A deathly quiet settled on the men and they glanced nervously at one another. After interminable seconds the pinging started up again.

"Damn," said Rodin. He thumped the console with his open hand. The sound of the ping softened to indicate the sub's escape from the tight circle within which the Kalnikov depended for the accurate delivery of its ordinance. The enhancements on the screens started to diminish on the starboard side and Rodin issued a terse order to follow. Perspiration coursed down his forehead and a drop, which teetered on the end of his nose, went unnoticed. Over the ten years of his command this was the first real encounter and he could not allow the sub to get away. The Kalnikov's speed made it the pride of the Russian Navy and no U.S. submarine would get the better of them; not under his command. The sound of the pinging changed and a second row of enhancements appeared on the screen, then a third. The sonar tech looked up with an expression of incredulity.

"Something is going on, Captain. The instruments are recording false readings—I don't know what to make of it."

Rodin stared at the main compass on the console. The needle oscillated in wild, frantic sweeps and a sudden fear gripped his heart.

"There appears to be an electronic interference affecting the equipment, Captain," shouted the sonar technician.

Viktor Rodin experienced a sudden loss of confidence in the Kalnikov's ability to overcome its enemy.

∞∞

13

A Race against Time.

O'Malley's senses recovered enough for him to assess his position. He dangled from the chute straps about ten feet off the ground, which he could see in the periphery lights of the control room. The overhead cable appeared to be a power supply for a building. It extended from the top of a transformer situated next to the turbine building and stretched over thirty yards of open roadway to a new construction project. His downward trajectory and approach appeared to have placed him on course with a temporary cable erected for a new building—a fateful combination of bad luck and Murphy's Law.

The question of how to extricate himself flooded his mind with all sorts of probable solutions. For a few moments O'Malley needed to suffocate his paranoia. With time as the most important feature of his plan, a quick answer would be a lifesaver and he looked frantically around him. There appeared only one way out of the predicament. A brief struggle with the main clasps of the chute produced success and a fall of about ten feet. To reduce the impact of his landing on the paved street below, he pulled his body into a ball and initiated a backward roll as his feet hit the ground.

O'Malley landed in one piece without injury. He jumped up and ran, in a half crouch, toward the control room. A quick glance at his watch confirmed that the meltdown of the reactor would soon begin—seven more minutes remained. His knowledge of basic physics reminded him of the fact that once the meltdown process started there would be nothing which could stop it. A full blown catastrophe and the loss of many lives galvanized him into action. Operators were running in all directions, some with expressions of panic and others with a grim determination to get to the turbine building, or in some cases, to get away from the adjoining reactor area.

O'Malley confronted a group of men, gathered in front of the emergency lockdown door to the turbine section. He pulled out his badge and raised it above his head. "Get away from the doors. I'm an FBI agent—your facility is under cyber attack."

The men looked at him without comprehension. "What do you mean?" said one burly man who appeared to have some seniority amongst the group. "What are you doing on the premises—this is a restricted area."

O'Malley fired back his answer. "I don't have time to explain. Your facility is under attack and I have a special code which will open the emergency doors. Your system has been hacked by a hostile enemy and the feed water turbine has been shut down. Let me pass, please."

The men looked at him in disbelief. "How do we know you aren't a terrorist?"

O'Malley couldn't believe the ignorance at first but, after consideration of their dilemma, his sudden arrival did appear to be strange. He waved the badge in their faces. "We have been monitoring the attempts of a hostile computer, which is trying to gain control of this facility. If you don't let me past I will have to use force."

He reached to the shoulder holster under the left arm and pulled out the Glock revolver. The men retreated and allowed him access to the entrance. Merlin's code unlocked the emergency door and it rolled up into the overhead lintel. O'-Malley shot into the turbine room and made his way around the equipment housing to the far wall where he could see an electrical panel with a main reset button. He remembered the previous visit to the warehouse and Merlin's plan to kill him through a rigged main power switch. The men all followed and stood around him. When the burley operator saw O'Malley hesitate he pushed passed and pressed the reset switch. With immediate effect the huge turbine started up and the process of feed water supply to the reactor resumed.

The operator seemed none the worse for ware and approached him. "Sorry about the scene. It just seemed strange to us—we thought you might destroy the turbine if you got inside."

O'Malley gave him a wan smile. "Don't worry about it. Take me to your shift supervisor."

They left the turbine building and walked toward the control room. Out of the corner of his eye he spotted a light up in the sky and it appeared to be on a trajectory, which would bring it right over the plant. He recognized it to be the landing lights of an aircraft.

He turned to the operator. "Do aircraft usually come this close to the facility? Isn't that the Harrisburg airport over there?" He pointed to the area of sky above the airport a few miles to the east.

The operator looked at the oncoming lights and frowned. "It's not usual that commercial airliners fly over our plant."

They could hear the engines of the commercial jet as it drew closer to where they were standing. O'Malley experienced a shiver down his spine.

"Quick. I have a bad feeling about this. Get inside the control room," he said.

They ran into the control room of the facility as the sound of the engines grew louder and closer. The incident of the turbine became forgotten as O'Malley contemplated a new scenario. He looked up at the ceiling to see a camera focused on the position where he stood. The shift supervisor came over to them, his eyes large and round. "What's that noise and who are you?" He shot O'Malley an enquiring glance.

O'Malley produced his badge. "I am a special agent with the FBI and your facility is under attack. I think we are about to be hit by a commercial aircraft."

The words no sooner out of his mouth were followed by an explosion, which threw the three of them to the floor. The entire front, concrete facade of the control room with its large windows caved in as the airliner struck the building. The last thing

O'Malley heard before he blacked out was a second explosion when the airliner's fuel tanks blew.

*

The Lear jet landed safely at Harrisburg Airport and rolled to a stop in front of the single hanger rented by the FBI. MacDonald, Martinez and Gabby poured out the exit door and ran to the main airport terminal. On arrival MacDonald went straight to security and presented his badge. "We need a vehicle right now," he said.

The security chief hesitated, squinted at the badge and threw a bunch of keys across the counter. He pointed to an SUV outside the building. "Bring it back in one piece," he instructed.

The three team members raced outside and clambered into the vehicle. MacDonald took the wheel and they sped off toward the island's closest power station entrance. It took five minutes for them to arrive at the bridge and cross the Susquehanna River, onto Three Mile Island. As they crossed the bridge they heard the sound of a low-flying jet, approaching the island from their right.

Martinez, who sat in the front passenger seat looked out his window and saw the landing lights of a commercial airliner descending toward the power plant. "That jet is aiming for the facility. Step on it, Roland."

A Boeing 727 flew over the top of their vehicle as they turned off the bridge. They raced down the road to the center of the plant area and held their collective breath as the aircraft descended lower. Visions of 9/11 came back to their minds as their vehicle raced toward the center of the buildings behind and below the jet. Visions of carnage and death corralled their thoughts.

Gabby teared up as she contemplated O'Malley's predicament. He might be in the direct path of the jet. A lump in her throat strangled the moan she desired to vent. MacDonald and Martinez stared, as if mesmerized by the scene.

The airliner plowed into the control center with a huge explosion of fire, flying parts and masonry. The roof of the building collapsed as did the entire front entrance. It may have been a small consolation to the building's designers that they specified the most stringent specifications of any structure ever built to the control room's construction. All sorts of scenarios from fires to bombs were taken into consideration. The synopsis of the aftermath done at a later date would testify to the strength of the design. The aircraft would not be so fortunate.

MacDonald brought the SUV to a screeching halt about one-hundred and fifty yards from the crash site. The aircraft's impetus took it beyond the control room as it plowed through several ancillary systems related to the generation of power. The power plant's fire control arrived; three fire trucks and two ambulances. Several blazes covered the control room area and the heat became prohibitive.

The fire crew raced to set up hoses and within minutes concentrated a deluge of water on the hotspots. MacDonald looked around him and felt at a loss. Martinez took the initiative and pointed to the turbine building. "The boss might be over there. That's where the initial problem was."

The three ran over to the turbine section and searched the building. An operator came running out of the reactor area and spotted them. "Who are you and what are you doing here," he asked.

MacDonald produced the FBI badge. "We're looking for our boss," he said.

A glimmer of recognition crossed the operator's features. "Oh yes, we met him a few minutes earlier before the jet hit us. It's just like 9/11 all over again—just on a smaller scale."

Gabby grabbed his arm. "Did you see what happened to our boss?"

The operator looked at his feet and appeared reluctant to answer the question.

"Where is he? Did you see him leave here?" Martinez shouted.

The operator looked crestfallen. "I saw him walk over to the control room with one of our senior operators moments before the jet approached the plant," he said.

They ran back to view the control room. Several of the emergency crew struggled to bring the fires under control while others sifted through the rubble for survivors. The damage to the building, inclusive of some minor collateral damage on each side, did not appear as bad as anticipated. The power station's control system switched to a backup computer situated in another area of the plant to prevent the stoppage of important and critical functions. The Reactor cooling and feed water systems, now fully restored by the restart of the turbine, continued to cool the overheated reactor. O'Malley's timeous arrival on the scene prevented a disastrous meltdown of the core.

Gabby ran toward the rubble to lift fallen roof timbers and kick aside debris in an effort to find

O'Malley. She called his name and in desperation petitioned two of the fire fighters, to attempt lifts of the heavier roof beams. They refused and tried to calm her down. "There's a forklift coming, ma'am. It will do all the heavy lifting you need."

She stood aside and wiped tears from her eyes. MacDonald tried to console her while Martinez scowled. "He did what he needed to do. He saved a lot of lives tonight— a reactor meltdown would not have done Harrisburg any favors."

The forklift arrived and began lifting the heavy beams and bits of masonry. After an hour they managed to clear the front entrance and then started on the central area. With the boom of the forklift extended, the forks turned over a section of roof. Underneath the debris they found three bodies.

∞∞

14

Diplomatic endeavors at the White House.

Ambassador Wang produced a handkerchief from his pocket and wiped his brow. The tension in the Oval Office became palpable as he leaned forward with a frown. "Mr. President, your rogue submarine sank one of our most up to date submersibles. There are all sorts of implications regarding the missiles and the reactor. These will have to be located and raised or somehow neutralized. The loss to our fleet is something the Chinese Navy can bear but we will require help with the cleanup."

The president removed his spectacles and cleaned them with a tiny cloth. "We will offer what help we can Mr. Ambassador but right now this rogue submarine is causing us a headache we could well do without. Until it is sunk there is not much more we can do. I am instituting a state of emergency today, throughout all of the United States. Merlin has attacked our banking sector and

Wall Street. Our homeland security is on standby to quell any trouble that will certainly arise due to the AI's actions."

"We understand the problems this Dr. Jones has caused your country, Mr. President but I need to know as soon as possible how the U.S is going to approach the sinking of the Yangtze"

The president's mind, occupied with all the other problems wanted to get Wang out of the room. He needed to concentrate on the next step, after the announcement of a state of emergency.

He no sooner got rid of the Chinese ambassador than the secretary informed him of the Russian envoy's presence. "What do the Russians want now," he complained.

The Russian ambassador, a short, stocky man with a beard, greeted the president with cordiality. "We are sad to hear about the financial distress the AI is causing your country, Mr. President. Our Premier offers his sincere regrets and wishes you well in the measures you are taking to stabilize the situation."

"Thank you, Sergei. I'm not sure how stabilizing a state of emergency is but it is the correct thing to do. What brings you on this visit?"

"We have news of your USS William Taft, Mr. President. One of our destroyers has come across it in the Pacific. They are dropping depth charges as we speak. We hope to resolve the matter for you and if we do—we are asking for a concession from your government."

"What are we talking about here, Sergei?"

"We are looking for your support in our annexation of the Ukraine."

"The Ukraine is an important NATO ally. Congress will never agree to it."

"Our Premier feels you will be able to influence them, Mr. President. The American people will be grateful to the Russians for dealing with this devastating problem you have—it should be remembered and rewarded. "We already virtually own the Ukraine, anyway."

"I'm not making any promises, Sergei. If you can sink the Taft, do so. But if you don't, the United States Navy will find it and deal with it."

"I will bear your sentiments to our premier, Mr. President. Tomorrow you will awake and the Taft will no longer be a problem. I bid you a good day, sir."

The ambassador left and Eli Marion entered. "I see the Russians paid us visit. What did they want?"

The president stood at one of the oval office windows and looked out across the green lawns. "Pompous little bugger. They want the U.S to support them in the annexation of the Ukraine. They have a destroyer out in the Pacific which he believes is going to sink the Taft."

Marion laughed. "Like the Chinese tried to do and failed."

The president's face reflected sadness. "I keep thinking of Bill Lowell and his crew. It must be so heartbreaking to face that situation. I know he'll do everything in his power to send the Taft to Davy Jones' locker."

Eli rubbed his chin. "We have some news of Merlin. I just heard from James Ingram that his special agent, the one who was originally involved on the SWAT team, was contacted by the AI. It seems that Jones has eliminated all the other original members and this O'Malley is the last one left."

The president's eyelids narrowed. "Ironical this O'Malley is now the agent who is vested with the mission of tracking Merlin down."

Eli nodded. "It's as though the AI is playing some sort of sick game with O'Malley and is tempting him into situations, to kill him. The latest prank could have extremely devastating consequences for us—I didn't want to tell you because you have so much on your mind already."

"What are you talking about, Eli? Never hold out on me because you think I'm overloaded."

"It's Three Mile Island, sir. Merlin has given O'Malley the task of saving a melt down on one of the reactor's if he can get there on time. According to one of O'Malley's team members, who reported the issue to Ingram from Harrisburg, the AI is going to shut down the feed water to the cooling system. We have no further news. Homeland security has been informed and are on it."

"Why did O'Malley not report it right away?"

"Merlin gave him no chance to do so, sir. The AI caused a communication blanket over the entire area. He got to the power station only just in time to prevent a meltdown of the reactor."

The president sat down at his desk and shut his eyes. "This is turning out to be real nightmare, Eli. I hardly recognize the state of our affairs since yesterday. It reminds me of that old Beatles song, 'Yesterday, all my troubles seemed so far away...'"

Marion turned to leave. "Bear up, sir. This too shall pass. I will keep you informed about Three Mile Island."

*

Captain Rodin stared at the instruments on the console panels. All the instruments appeared to be malfunctioning. He asked himself how this could be. His second lieutenant came up with the answer. "The supercomputer, the one who has taken over the American submarine, is doing this. It must have hacked our systems."

"What do we do?" Captain Rodin asked.

"We get the hell out of here, sir."

"And lose this magnificent opportunity to gain a swift victory?"

"We can't fight a war without our instruments Captain. If we don't bow out the American sub could sink us. If we leave now we live to fight another day."

"I know you are talking sense, but the war minister is banking on us sinking the Taft. He says he will use it as pressure to gain concessions from the U.S. president."

It is a great risk for us, Captain. The Taft has already sunk a Chinese attack sub."

"—because the Chinese bit off more than they could chew, Lieutenant. We have the most modern, feared anti-submarine destroyer in the world. Must we run from a fight—we have the sub on the run. I have an idea. We will turn off all our computerized systems and run as much of the ship on manual applications as possible. We have the Taft's present depth and direction. We will drop right back and make the AI think we are giving up the chase. If we ping only occasionally we may find that it will no longer continue to disrupt our instruments."

The Kalnikov slowed its speed to twenty knots and turned off as many computerized applications as possible. The Taft's passive sonar picked up the Kalnikov's immediate break-off of contact and the disturbance of instrumentation stopped. After an hour the destroyer switched on its computerized systems again and stayed at a distance. The occasional ping confirmed the Taft's position. Captain Rodin wanted to keep the sub in the Kalnikov's sights.

The hours passed by and daybreak came to cheer up the sailors after their long night's vigil. Captain Rodin spent most of his night brainstorming the possibilities of how they could sink the Taft. The Sub kept a steady pace at the sonar's extreme range and with their superior speed, they would be able to catch it within a few hours,

Four of his officers felt confident the Kalnikov could be run on manual applications without any problem, thus averting the problem caused by disrupted computerized systems. With the arrival of daylight the Falcon, their small reconnaissance helicopter, could fly and keep them on track. It would become their compass. The difficulty would be finding the sub's depth. The helicopter pilot would be able to see up to a certain depth but once the sub surpassed that it would not be of any help.

With a final question Captain Rodin made up his mind. "Who would like to earn the medal of courage for Mother Russia?"

All the officers raised their hands and grinned. Rodin contemplated them for a few moments. "You are all fine seaman. I know you will not let Russia down when we face the enemy. Get to your battle stations."

The officers all rose with one accord, saluted their captain and left in high spirits. Rodin followed but stopped to study himself in the mirror at the entrance to the officer's mess. He pictured the premier pinning the medal to his chest and then what it would look like as others observed it. The

medal of courage was the highest decoration anyone could receive and although it wasn't a Navy
medal, the premier awarded it when its recipients
involved themselves in extreme acts of bravery.

He stepped onto the bridge and gave the order
to continue at full speed. The technician turned on
the sonar and smiled. "We are right on course,
Captain."

Three hours later they came in range of the Taft
and turned off all their computerized equipment.
The Falcon took off from the back of the ship and
rose up into the sky. The pilot acknowledged after
a while that he could see the submarine, which appeared to be at a depth of thirty fathoms and traveling at a speed of 22 knots, well below its maximum. Rodin knew the Taft's active sonar would be
switched off. The destroyer's sonar picked up zero
pings on their hull which meant the sub's commander would be on passive detection.

Rodin made a comment, audible enough for
the seamen close to him to hear. "Now that we
have you in our sights again, Mr. Merlin—we will
not let you off the hook."

∞∞

15

O'Malley, the Hero.

Gabby, MacDonald and Martinez looked in horror at the scene. Three bodies lay exposed by the machine's forks, buried in the rubble. Gabby rushed forward and started to dig with frantic urgency, all the while calling O'Malley's name. Mac-Donald and Martinez joined her in an effort to move the heavier beams of roofing.

"Anyone got a rope?" shouted MacDonald.

A short piece of rope appeared and with the help of a fireman MacDonald attached it to one of the forks. He looped the other end around a heavy beam that straddled the three bodies and gave the sign to the operator to raise the forks. The beam moved and Martinez swung it out of the way. They dropped onto their knees to check the first body— the supervisor. MacDonald called the fireman to his side and indicated the need for a resuscitation attempt. Martinez rolled the second body over and felt for a pulse but received no confirmation of life. The operator, who helped O'Malley in the turbine room no longer lived. MacDonald's heart thumped like a base drum as he turned over the third body. He recognized the jacket—it belonged to O'Malley.

The special agent's body lay close to the operator's and it became clear the larger man had taken the brunt of the fallen beam. O'Malley's ashen face conveyed the worst but MacDonald would not give up on him and pulled the head into position to render artificial respiration. Gabby knelt at her boss' side. She took his hand, held it to her cheek and tried to remain calm. Interminable time passed as MacDonald breathed into O'Malley's lungs and pumped the chest with his hands. It paid off.

A splutter emanated from the FBI man's lips and he started to cough. MacDonald turned the head to one side as O'Malley puked. Gabby gave a shout of joy and kissed the dusty, blood-streaked forehead. Merlin's little game had not paid his master any dividends. The power station reactor did not suffer a melt down and O'Malley would live. She made a silent promise: not to allow the man she admired and loved, to be exposed to the wiles of the AI again.

*

The bright overhead light blinded O'Malley as he tried to open his eyes. His last recollection brought back the image of the roof of the control room caving in above his head. Bits of ceiling fell towards his uplifted eyes and then everything went dark. After several attempts he managed to keep his eyes open for a few seconds and caught the image of a woman's face, peering down at him.

"Wake up, Mr. O'Malley."

"Where am I?" he croaked.

"You are in the Harrisburg hospital," she said.

For a moment he couldn't put it together but as things began to fall into place he felt a surge of panic and tried to sit up. The nurse pushed him down. "Take it easy, Special Agent. You won't be going anywhere for a little while."

"But the power station...."

Another figure came into view, the face of a man. "Lie still, Mr. O'Malley. The power station has been secured and everything is under control."

"Who are you and what day is it?" asked O'Malley.

"I'm a senior surgeon at the Harrisburg hospital. You have suffered a concussion but everything is going to be fine. It's early morning, following the incident at the power station, which took place just before midnight."

"What about the supervisor and the operator who were with me?" O'Malley asked.

"You'll have to ask your colleagues, who are waiting outside the ward to see you." The doctor motioned to the nurse. "Tell them they can come in now."

Gabby rushed in ahead of MacDonald and Martinez. She grabbed O'Malley's hand and kissed his forehead. "Thank God you're okay, Dillon."

MacDonald's head peered over her shoulder. "Welcome back, boss. When we heard you'd returned to the control room with that operator, we thought the worse."

Martinez, not to be outdone, came around the other side of O'Malley's bed. "Good to see you with your eyes open, boss. You gave us all a fright."

"What happened to the supervisor and the operator who were with me when the jet hit?" Everything started to come back to him.

The three team members looked at one another. MacDonald took the lead. "The supervisor is here in the hospital and is expected to make it. Unfortunately, the operator didn't."

O'Malley became quiet and averted his eyes away from their stares.

"You saved the day, Dillon," said Gabby. "There is always some collateral damage, you know that. At least the reactor didn't melt down."

Martinez chipped in. "Yeah, boss. Merlin's little caper to inflict radiation on the city, failed."

O'Malley turned to Martinez. "Merlin's mission was not really aimed at the Harrisburg community, Diego. He was after me—to get me into a place where he could kill me. Don't forget—I'm the last remaining member of the SWAT team that killed Jones' family."

"By mistake," scoffed Gabby. "That weasel Dr. Jones is as twisted as a wire cable."

What about the airliner?" O'Malley asked.

"It was inbound from San Francisco with only ten people aboard. They were all killed in the crash."

Someone standing at the door of the room coughed and they all turned their heads. O'Malley shut his eyes when he recognized the person—his wife Janet.

MacDonald and Martinez greeted Janet and stepped away from the bed to allow space for her to greet her husband, but Gabby remained. She still clutched O'Malley's hand in her own.

Janet glared at her and said, "Do you mind?"

Gabby held her gaze and the obvious animosity showed, "Not at all."

She let go of O'Malley's hand and stepped aside, all with slow deliberation.

MacDonald intervened. He looked at Gabby and Martinez. "We should go and get some coffee."

They agreed and filed out of the ward.

Janet placed her hand on her husband's forehead and forced a smile. The tears welled up in her eyes and she bent down to kiss him on the lips. "How are you feeling, my love?"

"I'm bearing up, honey, and you?"

"Your boss called me at my mother's to say there had been an aircraft accident at the island and you were injured. I was lucky and managed to get a flight to Harrisburg, as a stand-by."

"Glad you could make it, hon," said O'Malley.

"What happened? Were you on the plane that crashed?"

"No. It's a long story. I did fly in, though—to prevent the sabotage of a nuclear reactor at the power station and I happened to be in the control room when the aircraft crashed into it."

Janet subdued her voice. "Don't you think it's time you took up on a new career, Dillon?"

O'Malley frowned. "This career is my life, honey. I would be useless at anything else."

She smiled and nodded. "You are one of the smartest people I know, Dillon. There are dozens of occupations you could walk into tomorrow, if you wanted to."

"That's precisely why I work for the FBI, sweetheart. They need people like me to protect the country."

She teared up. "You don't care about me or your son, Dillon; just your job and that, that..."

"What, Jan? You mean 'that woman?'"

"Yes—that woman. I can see the two of you have a special bond and it goes beyond work."

O'Malley groaned within himself. "It's not like you think, sweetheart. She is an associate, a colleague who happens to be an excellent agent. I need her on my team because she is one of the best."

Janet stood and released his hand. "And what am I to you, Dillon, chopped liver? I think she's more than that to you."

"It's all in your mind, love—please drop it now. I'm in no mood for a fight."

Janet looked crestfallen and bereaved. "I'm sorry, darling. I know you are recovering from your trauma and I didn't mean to start a scene."

"Come here," he said. He stretched out his arms to her. "I love you, Jan, you know that."

Janet snuggled up as close as she could and sobbed. He stroked her hair and spoke soothing words of comfort. After a while she sat up.

"I have to go now. Steven is alone at my mother's and he will be wanting lunch."

"How's he doing?" asked O'Malley.

"Fine—he misses his dad and wants to know when you are coming to visit."

"Tell him his dad is involved in a very important case and will come to visit at the first opportunity."

Janet kissed him on the forehead and said goodbye. When she got to the door of the ward she turned and caught his eye. "Don't let her into your heart, Dillon." She turned and left.

*

O'Malley awoke from a nap and found Gabby sitting at the bedside. "What time is it?" he asked.

She glanced at her watch. "It's 1:00pm. Mac-Donald and Martinez have flown back to D.C. Ingram wanted a full report."

"I can't lie here anymore. We must get back to work."

Gabby frowned. "Ease up. Dillon. The doctor says you need bed rest. You aren't going anywhere."

"I'm being serious, Gabriella, get my clothes."

"You have a concussion for Christ's sake. You'll do yourself damage."

"It not major—I'll be fine. Beyond a mild headache I'm feeling good, so get my clothes, Gabby. That's an order."

O'Malley understood her angst but he couldn't bear another minute in the ward.

"You're the boss," she said. "I hope you know what you are doing."

His clothes, brought in by a member of the theater staff, awaited pickup by the hospital laundry for cleaning and they lay crumpled on the floor, next to a chair. As Gabby bent over to pick them up, she frowned. "Do I have to bear the smell of these? They wreak of smoke— as though they've been through a war."

"Just give them to me." He sat up, moved to the edge of the bed and grabbed them from her. She moved to his side as he stood up and helped him onto his feet. A sudden rush of dizziness overtook him and he sat down.

In the moment of his blackout he saw the image of Bob Coulson again. The assassin mouthed the word to him as before. He shook his head and the vision disappeared.

"You see? Don't say I didn't warn you," chided Gabby.

O'Malley tried to stand for a second time and leaned against her, aware of the touch of her skin on his own. For a brief moment, their eyes met but before the inevitable could happen, Gabby looked away and rested her forehead on his shoulder. "I'm sorry, Dillon."

He took her head in his hands and kissed her on the forehead. "Help me get dressed."

"What did your wife say to you?" she asked.

"She senses that we have a closer than normal relationship."

Gabby looked up and her soft, brown eyes held his gaze. "What does a 'closer than normal relationship,' mean?"

He looked out of the window. "I haven't found an adequate definition for it just yet."

She chuckled. "You'd better find one before we both go bonkers."

With O'Malley dressed they walked to the floor's duty counter and he signed himself out. The nurse gave him lip about his current condition but he pulled out his badge and said, "FBI business, my dear."

Ten minutes later they were in a taxi on their way to Harrisburg Airport. Gabby called FBI headquarters on her cell phone and asked for the return of the corporate jet.

*

James Ingram lowered his chin and eyed O'-Malley. "Are you sure you should be up and about?"

"I'm okay, boss. We can't afford to allow one moment slip by in this investigation, and besides, we're shorthanded as it is."

"The president is pushing me for answers. What are you plans, Dillon?"

"I think I can use Jones' obsession with me, as the last standing member of the SWAT team, by issuing Merlin a challenge."

"That could be very dangerous," answered Ingram.

"Could things be any more dangerous for me than they are?"

"You have a point but you will need to be careful. Jones is no idiot."

"I'm aware of that, sir. But we need to discover where Merlin's lair is."

"I am concerned for your safety, Dillon. How do I explain to the director I allowed you to self-destruct? Allowing you to deliberately bate Merlin is the same as signing your death warrant."

"We have little choice, sir, but thanks for the sentiment. I assure you I'll take every possible precaution."

O'Malley left the assistant director's office and headed for his own. After a few minutes of contemplation he opened up his email and revisited Merlin's message. He searched the IP address and found it belonged to someone who worked for a grocery chain.

"Typical Hack" he mumbled.

He clicked on "reply" and began to type:

"This is for you, Merlin...."

∞∞

16

The Taft in Distress

Bill Lowell listened to the noise of the descending depth charges. The hydrophones picked up the initial splashes and the escaping air bubbles as the charges pierced the water's surface and burrowed down into the murky depths of the ocean. Each crew member stopped what they were doing and strained audio faculties to the limit. Eyes darted in all directions. Some perhaps entertained the hope the entire scenario would disappear, or they would wake up in bed on shore leave. Up to this point, the crew occupied their time in the monitoring of instruments and collection of data streams, which they knew would never be used. Everyone prepared themselves to experience a quick end.

The sonar supervisor, at intervals commented on the current estimated depth of the charges. As they drew closer to the Taft's depth, the expressions on the faces of the crew became more intense. The tension reached an almost unbearable level for some of the younger members and one started to weep. Lowell moved over to the seaman, a youngster of nineteen, and placed a hand of comfort on the man's shoulder.

"Lead charge at three-hundred fathoms, Commander."

Merlin took the Taft to three-hundred and twenty-five fathoms. Lowell calculated the time remaining in his head—the lead charge would be at their level within thirteen seconds.

"Hold on, the barrage is about to begin," he said.

The two charges exploded below the Taft's level—the first, at three-hundred and forty fathoms. The shockwaves shook the submarine with enough concussion to alter its direction. The second charge, set a bit shallower exploded above the sub, close to its mid-section and caused a section of steel plate on the sail, to buckle. For a moment Lowell envisaged a breach of the tower's integrity, but the plates held firm.

"Round one to Merlin," said Lowell.

A few seconds later the next barrage came. "Two more charges in the water, Commander—twenty fathoms and falling."

Merlin took the sub into a sudden dive, which caught everyone unaware. The chief planesman shouted his exasperation "What does the AI think it's doing—we are almost at crush depth and we're diving."

"I believe Merlin has already assessed the Taft's capabilities," said Lowell. "2300 feet is the designated crush depth for the OHIO class boat but the truth is no one knows what the real crush depth of the Taft is. There are some available parameters which Merlin might have used to estimate it."

"We're at four-hundred fathoms, sir," shouted the sonar supervisor.

"There we are—we're at the crush depth. I wonder what the commander of the destroyer is thinking?'

A young technician, with his eye on the hull integrity readings, responded. "We are starting to take water in the forward torpedo compartment, sir."

Lowell rushed over to observe the instrument. "Damn. That might derail our plan," he muttered.

"The pumps will be useless at this depth, Commander. If it gets bad the AI will have to bring us up, closer to the surface."

"Charges at three-hundred and eighty fathoms, sir."

The next round of depth charges began to explode above the Taft's position and the control center shook violently. Everyone held on for dear life.

"More charges in the water, sir."

"The destroyer's captain is aiming to release his entire arsenal on us. The shockwaves could cause the hull to breach somewhere, at this depth."

The charges exploded without harm to the sub and Commander Lowell smirked. "The destroyer's captain is guessing now. He was almost spot on with the first charges."

The crew waited but apart from the occasional ping, silence reigned.

The Taft began a sudden ascent toward the surface. Everyone held onto whatever they could find to steady themselves. The junior planesman called out the depth. "Two-hundred and twenty fathoms, sir."

The sudden rise ended at thirty fathoms. The chief planesman raised an eyebrow. Merlin is playing with fire at this depth—a charge will blow us completely out of the water."

Lowell spotted a light come on amongst the digital communication indicators. "The VLF buoy has been released. The AI is going to communicate with the destroyer."

"I'd love to hear what Merlin is going to say to the commander," said the sonar tech.

"I doubt whether the AI is going to make an actual communication—rather the use of low frequency, to either jam comms, or disrupt their instruments," said Lowell.

"That makes sense," said the sonar supervisor. "Our active sonar is operating which means we aren't in stealth mode and their sonar is lighting us up like a star."

They waited for some time before the tech turned to Lowell. "I can't believe this. The destroyer is dropping back—they're giving up."

"Merlin has either hacked their master control or disrupted their instruments. I don't know whether to laugh or to cry," said Lowell.

The others all nodded in empathy. "It's a kind of double-edged sword, isn't it sir?"

"Bittersweet," said the chief planesman.

Lowell called through to Petty Officer Hunt. "What is the state of the torpedo room? I believe we started to take in water when we were at crush depth."

"I'm afraid the tubes are all flooded, Commander. Water leaked into the main compartment but I see Merlin has activated the pumps, now that we're under less pressure. It will take a few hours."

"I assume you have cancelled the maintenance detail?"

"Yes, sir, but as soon as the water is cleared we'll send them in to confirm the integrity of the tube doors."

"Let me know when your men are able to get in there."

Lowell didn't want to say too much as Merlin might pick up on their plans. He still awaited news of the plan to introduce the virus into the super-computer's domain—the one consideration that might give them some hope of escape.

"The VLF buoy has been retracted and the destroyer is now ten miles astern, sir."

Lowell moved over to the one bank of sonar consoles and checked the enhancements. "The poor bastard probably doesn't know how close he got to sinking us. I wonder if he's just playing possum or whether he intends to keep tabs on us from a distance."

"Time will tell, Commander," said the chief planesman.

*

Henry read through the program one more time. The years since MIT might have dulled the memory of his previous, and short profession, but it all came back with the writing up of the malware. The four years at college served him well. The two years after that served him better for a time, until the FBI almost caught him. Writing up industrial spyware for competing organizations, to gain an advantage over their competition became a lucrative endeavor until one of the opposition companies, caught on to the illegal activity. That's when the shit hit the fan and he decided to disappear for a while.

Satisfied his work could not be further improved upon, Henry downloaded the short program onto the memory stick and stuck it in his pocket. One of his colleagues, who understood a little about computers, took on the responsibility to search for an information gathering location for the introduction of the virus. A place from where it would automatically be uploaded to the master control computer's hard drive. It might work—it had to work. Beyond this attempt there remained but one solution: sabotage of the torpedo. He did not want to think about the virus not working; failure was not an option.

The colleague knocked on the side of the bunk and approached. "Henry? You done with checking the virus program yet?"

Henry sighed and nodded. "It's the best I can do. The Captain says if it only works long enough for us to disconnect certain key applications, we may have a chance of beating the AI. On the other hand, the system was built to be tamper proof, so I'm not sure we can do much if master control is only down for a short period."

"Cheer up, mate. You can only do what you can do," said the colleague.

"Have you found a place for me to upload my little package?"

"I have found a good place. It's one of a range of USB's used for loading food quantities in the galley. The cook will do it for us. He loads information after every meal and if the two are done simultaneously the AI may not pick it up as a threat."

"Sounds great," said Henry. He produced the stick and placed it in his colleague's outstretched hand. "May God be with you."

An hour later the cook completed his preparations for the second shift's meals and they were set out on the counter for the seamen to pick up. He keyed in certain information with regard to the quantities for his galley computer and attached Henry's memory stick. The program file was pulled up onto the screen but not opened. At the same time he loaded the data of quantities with the virus. It all went off without a hitch. After the master control accepted both files he pulled out the stick and pocketed it.

Henry's colleague stopped at the counter, which separated the galley from the dining room and caught the cook's eye. He received a wink in return, a signal of the deeds accomplishment. He felt like laughing. The great Merlin, the super, smart quantum computer and oppressor of submarine systems, would fall to a bunch of ordinary seamen. He couldn't wait to tell Henry of their success. The captain would congratulate them and when they got home they would receive recommendations for promotions and salary increases.

Henry smiled when told the good news. "Now we'll see who comes out on top. I just hope Merlin does not have an antivirus detection greater than what the general technology companies work with. I know the package I wrote will beat most of the well-known programs."

*

Nothing changed in the immediate operations of the submarine. The entire crew knew about the virus by legacy of the crew's gossip-vine. Everyone waited with eager anticipation for something dramatic to happen. Either there would be retribution if the AI picked up on the plan or the instruments would start malfunctioning and the operators could rip the control of the sub out of Merlin's quantum hands. If the tension amongst the crew could be measured, the unit of stress would have been off the chart.

Commander Lowell retired to his stateroom because he could no longer stand the nervous glances and dramatic mannerisms of the men in the control room. The officer of the deck knew what to look for with regard to the instruments and how to set all the controls to manual application when the time came. It appeared to take longer than usual. He knew Henry's program would not find an easy passage under Merlin's scrutiny.

The word came with finality. "Commander to the bridge."

Lowell shot out of the stateroom like a road-runner. He took the stairs, three at a time and ar-rive on the bridge to see the operators staring at the overhead screen. He read the message:

"Your attempt at sabotage is noted, Comman-der Lowell. Clever, but certainly not enough to defeat my antivirus system. It didn't even cause a ripple. You will be punished. I do not intend to kill you yet, as my master wants to use you one last time to inflict misery on the families and the gov-ernment of the United States. This time is coming soon as we will be in a position to fire off all the warheads at once."

The faces of the operators in the control center reflected malevolent hate. One junior seaman ran off the bridge and down the stairs, sobbing. An-other placed his face in his hands and cried. Lowell did not know what to say, so he turned on his heel, stalked off the bridge and returned to his state-room.

∞∞

17

Trouble at the White House

President Barrow read the secret service brief for a second time. He found it difficult to believe the rumor with regard to certain powerful members of his government who wanted to replace him. What could any president have done different, given the same circumstances? He pressed the buzzer to alert his secretary. She popped her head around the door. "What can I do for you, Mr. President?"

"Tell Eli to haul his ass in here immediately."

She scurried off to find the Chief of Staff and several minutes later, Eli Marion walked into the Oval Office, concern written all over his face.

"Looking for me, Mr. President?"

Barrow flung the brief across the desktop and indicated Marion read it, which he did. After the first few lines he looked up and caught the president's eye. "This is bullshit, Mr. President. Where in God's name did they get this stuff from?"

"I don't know, Eli, but people will think where there's smoke, there will be fire."

"I don't doubt that but this rumor is totally unfounded."

"I want you to make contact with all these names on the list and indicate your concern with the way things are going in the country and with this administration. See if you can get any of them to confide in you."

"You want me to play the disgruntled, disenchanted victim?"

"You're good at that, Eli."

Marion cast his chief a dark look and the president forced a weak smile.

"I know you're loyal, dammit, but I know how you dislike my foreign policy regarding the Israelis—it's written all over your face every time I deal with your countrymen."

Marion looked hurt. "Does it really show that much, Mr. President?"

"Don't worry about it—just do as I ask."

"I'm right on it, sir," said Marion. He gave a short bow, turned and left.

*

Eli Marion loved his job. His dance with the Barrow administration started with a job as an aid to the secretary of state. Over the course of twelve years his rise in the ranks to the lofty position of chief of staff astounded most of his colleagues. With Arthur Barrow the road always seemed complicated, never easy, but he liked the president and got on well with him. Barrow's statement of Marion's dislike for certain political attitudes when it came to his home state of Israel rang a bell of truth. Barrow, an atheist, could see no practical use for religions of any kind. He tolerated the Jews because there were so many of them in his administration, however, Barrow would always be fair and honest with everyone. The previous president, dubbed as the most unpopular U.S. leader of all time, became known as a paragon of unfair practices and secretive, sexual indulgences.

Marion would do everything in his power to make sure Barrow stayed in the presidency. His own job depended on it. The brief, sent to the Oval Office by the secret service, shocked Marion to the core. In his mind Barrow exemplified good management, strong foreign policy and strong military strategy. This move, to have him replaced because of the present situation, smelled of a conspiracy. It stank of a low-down political ploy to take over the

Barrow administration. If that happened Marion knew he would lose everything he lived for.

The one person who could help him with inside information regarding the issue ran a business in Manhattan. This person, known to have shady dealings with the underworld but who also hobnobbed with members of congress, made it a practice to do favors for the gain of concessions in business. Aldo Banks possessed all the traits Marion hated but the man's usefulness could not be overlooked. A few concessions from Marion made Banks an ally, who saw the White House Chief of Staff as a powerful connection and a useful client to be in bed with. Banks took any opportunity to scratch the backs of D.C.'s influential patrons and Marion saw the association as a good political strategy.

He climbed into the back seat of the limo and gave the driver Banks's address. A quick phone call prior had confirmed Banks's availability. After ten minutes of heavy traffic they arrived outside the building and Marion waited for his driver to open the door for him. His mind raced ahead to think of a viable concession, which might attract Banks' involvement, in search of relevant information. Banks usually drove a hard bargain if the stakes supported it. The furniture shop looked like an old fashioned antique venture, which presented a great facade for the real business of drug trafficking. Marion knew about the shady dealings but his contacts in the FBI assured him the business remained low-key and provided mostly soft drugs to the many small-time addicts who stalked the streets of New York. He hated the drug business but Banks stayed below the threshold.

Banks stood with his back to the entrance in conversation with an employee. He heard the bell ring as Marion passed through the door.

"Eli, my old friend, how are you doing?"

"Good thanks, Aldo. How's business?"

"Business is great. Now what can I do for one of my most important friends?"

Banks sometimes patronized his clients but Marion tolerated it for obvious reasons.

"I need a favor, Aldo. It's political business as usual and I need you to be very discreet with any information I provide."

Banks dismissed the employee with a wave of his hand and beckoned Marion to follow him. They wound their way past stacks of antique furniture, ancient heirlooms, mirrors and desks, into a poky office with a single desk. Shelves, which lined one wall, contained reams of photocopy paper.

"Sit, my good friend. Tell me how I can help you."

Marion dusted the old wooden chair with a few sweeps of his hand and hoped he wouldn't require a tetanus injection by the end of the meeting.

"As I said, Aldo, this conversation never happened."

"Just as all our conversations are off the radar, Eli. You know I'll be discreet—now what can I do for you?"

Marion told him only what he felt was necessary. He wanted to know who might be involved in a conspiracy against Barrow.

Banks attended many functions where congress members titivated their fancies. He knew how to extract the information Marion looked for. Often the aides to politicians were the best to tap because they often picked up tit-bits from their respective bosses.

"I will see what I can do, Eli. This is dangerous stuff you are getting me involved in—it will cost you."

"I know you are a reasonable man, Aldo. I leave it in your hands. I will provide you with a little head start which will help you with business."

"I'll consider it a down payment," said Banks.

"The president will announce a state of emergency throughout the entire country today. You know what that will entail for your business and it should help you plan your affairs. There might be a run on the financial institutions."

Banks looked shocked. "You serious, Eli? Is this to do with some hacker and the banks?"

"It's much more than that, "said Marion. I can't reveal all the facts but a possible state of martial law could follow if the situation does not improve."

"Thanks, my old friend. I value this information most highly. I will get back to you as soon as I know something."

Marion thanked him and left. He told the driver to stop at his favorite haunt, a bakery that served Israeli delicacies with copious amounts of tea. The day still young, promised important news for America, which might turn the entire nation on its head.

*

The secretary of the treasury closed the door to her office and returned to her comfortable, leather chair behind the large mahogany desk. Opposite her sat a United States Air Force lieutenant general.

The secretary closed down the window on the screen of her laptop. "I see the secret service has picked up the rumors. I wonder how long it will take Barrow to respond."

The lieutenant general inspected his fingernails. "I'm sure it won't take long for him to react. I know he will quickly get into conference with that little rat, Marion. They'll try to cook up something before the evidence hits the media."

"I dislike getting my hands dirty, especially with a man like Barrow. Are you sure this plan will work?" she asked.

"Barrow may come across as a fair-and-square dealer of cards but when the evidence of his illegal deals surface—as trumped up as they are, the shit will hit his fan."

"And combined with the way things are going in the country he will be seen as inefficient and sterile as the last president," the secretary concluded.

The lieutenant general chucked. "This Dr. Jones couldn't have come at a better time for us. I know we still face a certain amount of uncertainty but I am assured by the FBI, they will eventually get matters under control."

"What if they can't overcome this computer? Meddling with the banks finances and Wall Street is one thing, but the abduction of a nuclear submarine is another kettle of fish altogether."

"According to the intelligence departments the sub isn't in position yet, where the AI can fire off the entire arsenal to hit the major cities of the nation. I'm assured by our friends in intelligence we will sink it before then. If we don't, the president said the commander, Bill Lowell, indicated the crew will do everything to sink it themselves. I think the odds are against this Dr. Jones."

"We would hope so. I've already made arrangements to move my family to a safer place," she said.

The Minister stood to leave. "Barrow will announce a state of emergency this afternoon. The 'evidence' of his crime and the incompetence of his administrative, will hit the media shortly after and the public will do the rest. Just sit tight until the congressional meeting next week. The media will be saying what a great president you'll make after they officially swear you in."

The secretary smiled. "I'll talk to you again tomorrow."

*

Marion read through the headlines of the newspaper at a phenomenal speed. Some said he could read an article of a thousand words in a few seconds. The current news read like an apocalyptic event and the media enjoyed a field day. The left wing fueled the charge against the Barrow administration, citing the non-existence of leadership in the face of the economic disaster which loomed.

So far, the news regarding the abduction of the USS William Taft remained as "lost at sea." The general public knew nothing of Merlin or the infamous Dr. Jones. The truth rested with the politicians and government security departments, who realized the panic such news would cause. They would keep the truth from the public's ears for as long as possible and if the first bomb fired from the Taft hit an American city, martial law would be proclaimed.

The state of emergency would set the scene for better control and until the arrival of more positive news, the government would prepare for riots and unrest. People did not respond well to the lack of finance. Several of the huge financial providers placed their internet bank facilities off limits, which made millions of people throw their toys out of the cot.

A leak to the media, with regard to the abduction of a nuclear submarine and the potential threat this posed to the world, would create havoc.

Marion speculated on the use of such a leak by powerful people. It would be devastating to any government.

∞∞

18

O'Malley and Merlin

O'Malley hit the enter key and waited. He tried to stay calm but a certain amount of nervousness caused his hands to tremble. His head felt as though it would burst and a physical weakness racked his normal vitality. The response to his message came within seconds.

"I wondered what happened to you, Special Agent O'Malley. After the arrangement of the accident at the power station I assumed you to be dead until I saw you and your female staff member at the hospital in Harrisburg. I congratulate you on your survival so far, but you won't last long because the odds are stacked against you. I see you are a romantic, Dillon. You have challenged me to a duel—just like two opponents in bygone times. I understand your strategy. You hope I will respond and reveal my location. It is too soon for you to know where my master and I are situated, but I admire your courage and so I will play along. The first move belongs to you."

The bold print jumped out at O'Malley. He could not have hoped for more from Merlin. A sudden pang of fear clutched at his resolve. Negative scenarios beset his drive to remain focused and clear. If the plan failed, he might have signed his own death warrant—however, with the die cast, he needed to make the first move.

Despite the occasional dizzy spell, O'Malley steeled himself for the task ahead. He called the team on their cell phones and arranged to meet in the briefing room. When the team arrived he asked them to be seated and outlined his plan. Martinez and MacDonald left after the talk. Gabby felt the bump on O'Malley's head.

"It's still a bit swollen but looks good." she said.

He gave her a lob-sided grin, popped more headache tablets and indicated they should be on their way. With Gabby behind the wheel of the Chevy they drove toward the Washington Metro rail line.

Gabby cast a sideways glance at O'Malley. "Are you okay, Dillon? You look pale."

"I'm fine, Gabs. Don't worry about me—if you must worry, then worry about what Merlin."

"How did you manage to arrange this new device you were talking about?"

"I called my old friend, Professor Wheeler at the Neuroscience Institute to see if there wasn't a way we could fight Merlin at his own game. As fate would have it he and his assistant, Samantha, are busy with a quantum communication system. I outlined our problem and they both thought we might be able to make use of their latest discoveries in instant particle communication."

"Any idea how it works?" she asked.

"Not really, but roughly speaking when particles become entangled, they have an instantaneous communication with each other. If you alter the spin of one, the spin of the entangled mate will automatically alter as a matter of course and there is no time delay between the two events."

"So, how do they intend to use this against Merlin?"

"By means of a device which will pick up on a quantum signals, the type Merlin uses, to hack other devices with. The device brings the particles in the signal into a superposition. Once the particles have become entangled it will be possible to trace the origin of the signal's originating content."

"That's brilliant," said Gabby. "You friends will set up the device for us?"

"The device has already been set up at Metro Center. It has a connection to the other stations down the line, so any signal Merlin sends to the transit will be picked up and tracked to its origin."

"What do we have to do?"

"Not a thing, really. Perhaps just hang on and hope the AI doesn't kill us."

"We are the bait?"

"Exactly. Merlin wants to kill me and the moment I appear on the station's cameras, he will know. I have asked him to meet me at Metro center to speed up the process. Merlin already knows where we are headed."

"A comforting thought," said Gabby.

"Here's the thing—it will only be me who gets onto the train—not you. I'm not placing your life in danger."

"You're kidding me, O'Malley. You know that's an absolute no-go."

"I'm afraid I insist Gabs and I'm sorry, but that's an order. You have to obey your senior agent."

"Not when he is busy self-destructing."

"That's the last thing I'm doing and you know it, Gabriella."

She turned her eyes toward him and smirked. "How come you always use my full name when you lay down the law?"

"Maybe because I have feelings for you and I don't want you in harm's way."

"I'm still coming with you, Dillon. I don't give a shit what you say."

"We'll see," he said.

"Yes—we certainly will," she concluded.

*

On arrival at Metro Station O'Malley purchased a ticket at the dispenser. Gabby sneaked off to another dispenser and bought her own ticket. They made sure to stand in full view of the cameras, which were situated in various places, to parade themselves before Merlin. A wait of ten minutes for the next train gave O'Malley time to purchase a coffee from the kiosk and Gabby enough time to badger him about her inclusion on the trip.

"I will be coming along; I bought a ticket," she taunted.

"Over my dead body," said O'Malley.

"I will simply stand in another place and get into another car. You won't be able to stop me."

In the end O'Malley saw the fruitlessness of his argument and relented. Happy to get her own way she stopped her tirade.

Ten Minutes later the train arrived and they selected a car. He had chosen a time when few people would require the service and hoped this consideration would reduce the potential collateral damage. O'Malley glanced at his watch—11:30 pm. The government's announcement of a state of emergency changed little for the locals. Few people understood the true depth of the crises. When the first missile fell the government would declare martial law and thirty of the most populous cities would need to be evacuated in an orderly manner. The military remained the viable option to accomplish the task.

Gabby cuddled up to O'Malley and rested her head on his shoulder. She struggled to keep her feelings for him under control and in consideration of his rocky marriage, tried not to put any pressure on him. She knew of his depression in regards to the loss of his daughter. Her own loss of a younger brother to drugs reminded her of the bitter struggle her own parents endured. It would also be expedient not to be the cause of a marriage breakup. Her own marriage to a member of the CIA had come adrift three years prior.

The train flew along the rails with twelve other travelers oblivious to the potential danger. O'Malley felt a twinge of conscience about it but there had been no time to come to any arrangement with the Metro rail authorities. He also did not want to alert Merlin to their real objective. The train traveled along at a fair speed under the power of its electric motors.

O'Malley considered spots along the line which might endanger their lives and a siding at Union Station came to mind. Gabby relaxed in relish of each moment spent with the man she loved. She didn't mind if he appeared oblivious to the way she felt about him. Their relationship would blossom at the correct time.

The train continued to accelerate. The people in the seats looked around with worried expressions, in ignorance of the looming danger. O'Malley shouted at them to hang on and he ran through to the lead coach. No lever or gadget existed for him to govern the speed.

"Go back and pull the emergency brake," he yelled.

Gabby instinctively obeyed and returned to the back of the lead coach, where she found the brake and pulled on it as hard as she could. The train, however, did not respond.

"It's not working," she yelled.

The train by this time had reached maximum speed on its approach to Union station. O'Malley's eyes searched ahead and as he watched, another three-coach combination pulled out of the siding, onto the line ahead of them. He stared hard before the realization hit him—the second train raced toward them, on a collision course.

O'Malley didn't wait. He raced back, grabbed Gabby by the hand and pulled her along behind him. His foot caught a bench support and they both stumbled to the floor. For a moment O'Malley lay stunned, unable to move. Gabby realized his predicament, grabbed him by the belt, yanked him onto his feet and the two of them took off, in an attempt to reach the back of the last car. The other people stared at them wildly and O'Malley shouted for them to get down under the seats.

The oncoming train did not have a great distance in which to gather its speed, but O'Malley's train traveled at maximum pace. When the collision came, it caused an ear splitting, metal grinding and glass shattering combination of sounds, which reverberated up and down the line. Fire broke out everywhere with the disintegration of the lead cars.

The middle cars on both trains fared better but crumpled in their centers and were derailed by the impact. The rear cars ended up buckled and broken at right angles to the track. The occupants in the back coach of O'Malley's train held on for dear life as their transporter bucked high into the air and buckled in several places, with the front end coming to rest on top of the middle car's rear end. When both mangled trains came to rest, the crackle of fire remained the dominant sound. No one screamed or cried out. The chaotic scene rested in silence.

*

MacDonald and Martinez ran as fast as their legs could carry them. O'Malley's plan placed the men in the correct place, prior to the disaster. They waited for the arrival of the train and when the sound on the rails informed of its approach they braced themselves for potential action from Merlin. When the train in the siding powered up with a sudden charge of energy and began to move forward, the men picked up on Merlin's plan—a catastrophic head-on collision between the two trains.

They sprinted down the track in the wake of the coaches which exited the siding and witnessed the crash from close quarters. It would be a scene never to be forgotten. Fire hindered a close up look of the lead cars but Martinez found a way around the wreckage and brought them closer to the twisted steel of the back coach of O'Malley's train. On approach of the tangled mess, anxiety increased as hope faded.

∞∞

19

Clash of the Titans

Captain Rodin cast an eye at the screens each time any of the sonar technicians turned the system on, to check for the submarine. The enhancements on the screens, indicating that the distance between the Admiral Kalnikov and the Taft had greatly diminished. The destroyer ran dark, without external lights and with every system on manual, to shut out Merlin's influence. No one on the bridge uttered a sound and the soft green glow of the backlit instruments illuminated the grim faces of the men. The captain and the sonar tech spoke in brief terms with regard to distance between the two vessels.

"Six miles, Captain. The submarine appears to have slowed its speed to about eighteen knots."

"Depth?" Rodin enquired.

"It remains steady at one hundred and fifty feet, sir."

"They must know we're gaining on them. Perhaps they are having some issues," commented Rodin.

"It's possible our charges caused some damage, Captain."

"—or the depth they sank to caused problems. I know the Taft is the strongest OHIO class submarine in the U.S. fleet. I think we might have missed them with the charges because they submerged passed the usual crush depth parameter."

The distance continued to diminish as the Kalnikov barreled onward. The sea became more tempestuous with mountain sized swells and wave crests, which smashed over the destroyer's bow to fling spray against the bridge's windshields.

"It looks as though we're heading back into a storm," ventured Rodin. "These conditions favor the submarine. If this gets worse, it's going to be a difficult battle for us."

The chief petty officer chipped in. "Do you think we should abort, Captain?"

"It would be senseless to run now, Yuri. We are about to inflict a great victory for mother Russia—let's not waiver."

"We are all ready to serve, Captain," said the petty officer.

The sonar operator called out. "Five miles, Captain—depth remains constant."

"I am going to my quarters. Call me when we are within one mile, or if the enemy makes any changes to its operation."

Rodin left the bridge and made his way down the corridor to his room. He felt sleep deprived and believed it would be beneficial to have ten minute power nap.

He slumped down onto his bunk and within a minute, fell fast asleep.

*

Bill Lowell stretched out on his bunk like a man in a daze, his eyes riveted to a spot on the ceiling. There remained one more chance to stop the Taft but it offered no hope for the survival of the crew. The water in the torpedo room, still posed a problem. He glanced at the bottom drawer of his desk. In its confines lay a colt 45 revolver. He could end his life right at that moment but the faces of his crew floated before his mind's eye, each appealing to the need for his presence. He represented their hope of calm stability and strength to face the final moments like men should. If he took the cowards way out there would be little hope the men would continue to push through with the plan and sink the Taft. Not that it mattered much, as death would come for all of them—unless God intervened with a miracle. Lowell fought off his depression and focused on the bedside photo of his family. He went through each face one by one—his wife and children, now all grown up, seemed so far away.

Merlin's words came back to him. What punishment awaited him and the crew? Would the AI change conditions on the sub? Increase or lower the ambient temperature, or turn off electrical power to the galley and thus disrupt their meal preparations? It all seemed so senseless.

A knock on the stateroom door brought the real world back with a bang. He shouted, "Come in, it's unlocked."

Chief Petty Officer Hunt opened the door. "There is a developing scenario, Commander. The destroyer appears to be back on our tail."

"I'll come to the control room," he said.

A few moments later Lowell stood behind the sonar supervisor and observed the screens. The oblong enhancements of light pulsated with a brightness against the green backdrops on each sonar screen and the sound of pings increased in intensity.

"It looks like the captain of the destroyer means business this time," said the sonar supervisor.

"I'm willing to bet he has turned most of his vessel's instruments to manual operation. Merlin won't be able to hack the master control and make all the instruments go crazy."

"The hydrophones reveal there is a heavy sea running, Commander."

"It won't make much difference to the depth charges. I think he might change his strategy this time, though. I think he will choose to cluster the charges at specific depths and use a hundred or more—lay down a barrage," said Lowell.

The chief planesman posed a question. "What do you think Merlin will do, sir?"

"That, my friend is the million dollar question." "We'll have to wait and see. The AI's program probably includes every possible scenario in sea warfare there is. There's not much a submarine captain can do when a destroyer is sitting almost on top of him, dropping mines."

The overhead screen lit up with a message. They all jerked their heads upward and waited. Lowell made a comment. "I guess Merlin wants to say something."

"You will have realized we are being pursued again by a destroyer. It is the same ship that attacked us earlier, a Russian attack destroyer by the name of the Admiral Kalnikov. The commander is Captain Viktor Rodin. I distracted them last time by sending out a VLF buoy which transmitted disrupting signals to their computer programs and instruments. They are now running manual applications so I will employ other tactics. I am letting you know all this so you can see nothing will be able to stop the holocaust to come. I will defeat all attempts to sink the Taft, and in particular, the ones you are planning."

The message ended with an emphasis on the final sentence. The men looked at Lowell who scowled as he considered the computer's statement. Did Merlin know of the plan, to use a torpedo battery in the sabotage of the vessel? It did not seem clear to him.

"I think the AI is messing with our heads," he said.

A few moments passed in the wake of his words before the sub's internal atmosphere experienced a sudden change. The air became humid and un-breathable.

The screen lit up again: *I promised you a pun-ishment.'*

The men all looked at each other and shook their heads.

The sonar operator made an observation. "The destroyer is now approaching, Commander. 1000 yards."

*

Captain Rodin steeled himself for action. The heavy sea swamped the destroyer at times and it became difficult to see through the deluge of water run-off, on the bridge windshields. All the seamen held onto supports wherever they could be found. The skies, black with thunder clouds and rain, cov-ered the ship like a blanket and visibility dropped to twelve-hundred yards.

The sonar operator called out the distances and depth, with monotonous precision and at regular intervals. The tension on the bridge rose exponen-tially as the enhancements on the bank of screens got brighter and the sound of the pinging, louder.

"I'm surprised he has not moved," said the second lieutenant. "He must know we are here."

The captain called for a decrease in the ship's speed and they slowed to a crawl. The shear roughness of the seas appeared to be on the increase as minutes dragged by. The Kalnikov continued to push through the tops of waves which would have caused havoc with a smaller vessel. Visibility reduced and the rain beat down on the windshields of the bridge with a vengeance.

The sonar tech made a sudden announced. "The sub is making a move, sir. It is turning sharply to port—twenty degrees."

Captain Rodin responded with an instruction for the helmsman, "Port—twenty degrees."

The Kalnikov wallowed in the trough of two huge swells and almost turned over like a turtle, but the vessel, built to stringent specs, righted itself again. They ran through the waves at an acute angle and each impact, sent lengthy vibrations through the hull. The younger sailors not used to such rough seas closed their eyes and hung onto their supports for dear life.

"Decrease speed by three knots," shouted Rodin.

The ship slowed further and he glued his eyes to the bank of sonar screens. The submarine changed its depth. Instead of a dive tactic it appeared to be making ready to surface.

*

The Taft made a sudden change to its direction and the crew, mere passengers, waited to see what Merlin would do. Lowell knew what he would have done in the circumstance. He would have crash-dived the Taft back to crush depth and risked the leaks, but the AI appeared to have other ideas. What Lowell couldn't see or sense was the heaviness and roughness of the sea at the surface. This knowledge would have changed his mind. What he also didn't know—Merlin could hear the Russian captain's broadcasts to the helicopter, which acted as the destroyers eyes. One of the broadcasted messages described the sea's surface from the air. It gave the speed and direction of the wind, all information Merlin could use in the decision of how to carry the fight.

Lowell looked at the panel of lights above the planesmen's console and noticed the initiation light of the VLF buoy.

The air in the submarine bordered on unbreathable. Perspiration poured down all the faces of the men in the control center, accompanied by fits of intermittent coughing. Some men succumbed to a state of semi-consciousness. They clung to life with each breath and kept their eyes glued to the screens.

The junior planesman called out. "We have moved twenty degrees to port, Commander."

The sonar supervisor followed. "The destroyer has turned twenty degrees to port as well, sir."

The two vessels continued to plough through the heavy sea in a cat and mouse symphony until the Taft initiated another sudden change. It did what no submarine commander in his right mind would do. To Rodin's astonishment, the Taft surfaced in full view of its pursuer.

"I don't understand—we'll be sitting ducks for their cannons. One direct hit from a six inch will send us straight to Davy Jones," said Lowell.

Petty Officer Hunt wiped the sweat out of his eyes. "I thought the end would come last time when the destroyer started with its depth charges but this is certainly a suicide move."

When the sail broke the surface everyone in the sub realized the extreme severity of the weather conditions. Lowell considered the wind speed to be close to that of a category two hurricane as the Taft turned to line up its stern with the destroyer.

∞∞

20

A Wild Goose Chase.

The wreckage of the rear car lay crumpled across the tracks. Martinez found his way around the mess of tangled steel and began his search for gaps in the steel carriage's side. The extreme wreckage of the middle and front cars negated any attempt to search for survivors. Several fires made it impossible to get close. The back car appeared to be the most viable spot for anyone to have survived. He stood and gaped at the scene until MacDonald, who followed in his wake, gave him a shove from behind.

"Come on, Diego. We don't have any time to waste."

They spotted a window which still retained most of its shape and moved toward it. MacDonald kicked out the glass and popped his head into the murky interior. No signs of any bodies could be seen through the film of dust and smoke. Fabric on one of the benches near the front end smoldered and threatened to burst into flames, which galvanized him back into action.

"Quick, Diego. This whole car is going to go up in flames. They have to be in here somewhere."

He dived through the small aperture and pulled himself along the line of benches, searching each gap in between for signs of life.

Martinez followed on behind as they traversed the length of what remained of the coach. MacDonald stopped to wipe the dust from his eyes and heard a moan. It came from beneath a seat to his left and he stuck his hand in to feel around on the floor. A hand grabbed his and he pulled. The face of a middle aged woman appeared, with hair all disheveled and face smeared with grime.

"Help this one out, Diego," he shouted. Martinez moved into position as MacDonald surged ahead toward the back of the car.

He touched someone's foot, which stuck out in his path. A quick search for the person's head produced an older man with gray hair. There appeared to be little MacDonald could do for him. Martinez helped the middle aged woman to crawl out from her position and pointed the way out. Despite the shock, she responded well and made her way toward the broken window while he followed in MacDonald's wake. Two other people whom MacDonald missed along the way were found and helped by Martinez, who pointed the way to the exit.

The cave-in of the roof close to the rear end of the car made it difficult for MacDonald to pass. He pushed up on the inside of the ceiling with all his strength and managed to make some space to maneuver his body through a gap. A noise emanated from a position near the back door, which had been jammed by the collapsed roof.

"What took you so long?"

Despite the seriousness of the situation MacDonald could not help express a grin. O'Malley's face appeared out of the gloom and the whites of his eyes gleamed in the fraction of available light. He lay on his back and appeared to be trapped by a body, which lay on top of him. Gabby lay full length over the top of O'Malley, as if in a last resort to provide some protection. MacDonald reached out a hand and shook Gabby's shoulder. Her head shot up and she looked around in amazement. "Are we alive or is this the place people go when they die?" she croaked.

MacDonald laughed in part at her joke, but more because she and O'Malley were still both alive. "I thought the plan was for you to stay at Metro Station, Gabby."

"You have to be kidding me," she said.

O'Malley tried to turn onto his side. "Give us a hand, Roland. Where's Diego?"

"I'm right here, boss," shouted Martinez.

It took another few minutes before the four agents managed to extricate themselves from the wreckage. Sirens wailed in the distance and people waiting at the station came at a run,to render assistance. MacDonald waived them toward the back car. Uniformed security arrived and then paramedics. A young woman checked O'Malley and Gabby over for injuries but both agents assured her they were okay. Several spectators gathered to observe.

"Let's get out of here. We've accomplished our mission and there's no doubt Merlin was involved up to his quantum eyeballs," said O'Malley.

They walked back to the station and out into the parking lot to MacDonald's car.

O'Malley asked Martinez for his phone. "Drive straight to Professor Wheeler's home. He'll be waiting to hear from us—let's hope the intrusion device he planted at the stations worked. It'll take us at least an hour. "I know Merlin is monitoring my phone but I doubt he would bother with yours," he explained.

He keyed in the professor's number and Wheeler answered. "We're on our way," said O'-Malley.

He turned to MacDonald. "Drive to Port Morris, New York. I'll guide you to the home when we arrive in the area."

*

They pulled up outside the professor's home on Locust Street, Port Morris at 2:30 a.m. The converted warehouse fascinated MacDonald and he uttered his appreciation of the professor's interior decorating abilities. Wheeler greeted them and they sat in the large open area, which contained most of the living area. A set of bay windows looked out onto the bay, where the Brother islands could be seen in the distance.

"You appear to have survived a war," said the professor.

"Something like that. It's been quite a hectic twenty-four hours, but we I believe we've accomplish what we set out to do."

The professor smiled. "You certainly did and my little quantum device worked like a charm. I traced the originating signal to a place in Queens, not too far from here. I'm pretty excited as to how efficiently it worked. The entangled particles reported an instant return."

"Well, don't keep us in suspense, Lucas—give us the address."

The professor obliged and O'Malley glanced at his watch. "I know time is of the essence, but we've all been going at it for more than thirty-six hours. I suggest we get some shuteye and make an early start in the morning. Can we use your spare room and couch, Professor?"

*

Early the next morning the four agents left the professors home and drove to Queens. The address turned out to be a small industrial concern, which rebuilt old computers. It seemed just the right sort of business Jones would have as a front.

MacDonald parked his vehicle in the street about fifty yards from the premises and they all got out.

"Let's be wary. Jones will probably have the place protected by all sorts of gimmicks, being the evil genius he is," said O'Malley.

They drew their weapons and advanced toward the front door of the building. A single glass-framed door with a sign-written company name, "Custom Computers & Co" appeared to be the main entrance.

"I'll go behind and see if there's a back entrance," said MacDonald. O'Malley, Martinez and Gabby approached the front door with care. O'Malley reached out with his free hand and touched the handle. To his surprise the door swung open.

""It's not locked," said O'Malley.

The early morning rays of the sun poked long tentacles of light across the dark sky as O'Malley pushed the door open.

"Don't switch on any lights, Dillon. Jones has probably got this place rigged to blow," said Gabby.

The interior still nestled in the twilight of the early dawn, which forced Martinez to produce a slim-line flashlight from one of his pockets. He poked his head inside the door to search the long passageway for any signs of beams, or trip wires and a moment later rejoined by MacDonald, and they slipped into the hallway.

"It looks safe so far. I don't see anything ominous, but keep your eyes peeled," said Martinez.

They moved into the hallway with slow deliberation and made their way down the passage, to the room at the end. A small office appeared on the right. Within its confines, through the gloom, they could see a desk and a filing cabinet. O'Malley crept toward the larger room, situated at the end.

He raised his hand and stopped. "I see a trip wire. It's set at the base of the door jamb and extends across the entrance."

"Too easy," said O'Malley. "There will be more —Jones is trying to tempt us. I say we vacate and call the bomb squad."

He pulled out his phone and looked up the number of the NYPD. After a short conversation he turned to the others. "They are on their way."

Martinez traced out the content of the room with his flashlight. Two workbenches, with tools and equipment, plus old computer components, gave an indication of Jones' presence. They returned to the smaller office and Martinez made another quick search for any hidden trip wires or beams before he stepped over the threshold and up to the desk. O'Malley followed and opened the top drawer. Gabby peered over his shoulder while MacDonald and Martinez scrutinized the various items on a shelf, against one of the walls.

"O'Malley pulled out a folder which contained paperwork. "Shine your flashlight over here, Diego. These look like invoices."

Martinez obliged and they squinted at the papers in the file, which O'Malley placed on the desk.

"There are material descriptions here I recognize—stuff required for a quantum computer," said Gabby.

O'Malley lifted out two sheets of paper. "Here's an invoice for ten cylinders of liquid nitrogen. It would be needed for the low temperatures under which the computer processor needs to operate. Here's another for the cooling system and refrigeration components."

Gabby lifted out another sheet. "This is for the circuitry."

Martinez made an observation. "I didn't see any sign of this stuff in the workshop, which means Jones has removed the computer to another area for its operation."

"So—we're still dead in the water," said O'Malley. "Jones knew we would try to pinpoint Merlin's position. I would think he sent the final signals from here and then left this workshop as a backup in case we escaped the railcar episode. He must have moved everything last night."

MacDonald cleared his throat. "This place is more than it looks. We gained entry too easily, which makes me think we'll have to be careful in leaving."

"You're right, Roland," said O'Malley. He indicated the need to retrace their steps to the entrance. The flashlight oscillated in a circular motion to reveal the floor, walls and roof in one sweep as Martinez stepped out into the passageway.

"Follow me," he said. They made their way toward the exit. A light, situated in the ceiling to one side of the entrance switched on with a sudden display of brilliance, and caught them in its glare. The surroundings illuminated with an instant brightness and they stopped in their tracks. A voice spoke to them.

"Well done, Special Agent O'Malley. I see you escaped Merlin's little ruse to eliminate you. I'm afraid you have lived out your luck, though."

A speaker and a camera, both mounted on the wall above the door, caught their attention while the voice continued to address them. O'Malley deemed the voice to be familiar, but he could not place it.

He regained his nerve. "You won't get away with this, Jones. You can eliminate us but you'll always be looking over your shoulder."

The voice hesitated for a moment and then Jones chuckled. "It will not make any difference after my revenge is complete. You and your government took everything away from me a long time ago. It's time you all paid for your heinous crimes."

∞∞

21

Uncovering a Conspiracy

Eli Marion read the secret service report with alarm. President Barrow would still be another hour with his family, time the president regarded as a priority. This news, however, could not wait and the Chief of Staff raced up the stairs to the president's private quarters. He didn't wait to be told to enter after a quick knock on the door but surged into the living room, to find the president and the first lady in deep discussion over morning coffee.

"My apologies, Mr. President but something important has come up—can we have a word?"

The president looked annoyed and glanced at his wife. "Can you give us a moment, love?"

The first lady rose with a smile and nodded. "It's time you got back to work, Arthur," she said.

She walked out of the living room and closed the door.

"What's so important that it couldn't wait for me to get to the office?" asked the president.

Eli handed him the report. "It has started."

The president read through the lines with a measure of haste and his features hardened. "Someone has leaked the news of the Taft's abduction to the press?"

"Not only that but the full story of what they call our 'government's complicity' in taking out Dr. Jones' family and his intent to take out his full revenge on the United States of America. The story of Merlin's intervention and disruption of our financial enterprises is also included."

"Is there any way we can stop the press from printing the story?"

Marion looked resigned. "We can do that but the story will be leaked to all the newspapers and not just one. It has already appeared on the internet, so we can't stop it."

The president threw the report down onto the coffee table. "I want to know who leaked this story. There are only a handful of people who knew all the details. In the meantime prepare the news room for a state of the union address. Invite all the journalists—we might as well give them the lowdown before the papers hit the street."

"I'm on my way Mr. President. I will send the speech writer to the office. You'll have about twenty minutes to marshal your thoughts before he gets there. We will set the media meeting for noon. I understand the press will run this in the evening news."

The president grunted his acknowledgment and Marion beat a hasty retreat. Once back in his own office he called the speechwriter for a quick brief. The media would be in for a frenzy of finger pointing, with Barrow's administration at the brunt of it. The speech writer needed to highlight the importance of peace and calm at a time of extreme uncertainty. The nation needed to be comforted and assured of the government's plans to overcome the obstacles and bring peace. The outcome of Dr. Jones' family drama remained the result of a previous administration's decision and this could not be blamed on President Barrow.

*

Aldo Banks raised his glass of whisky and toasted the gods of providence. His meeting with an old friend, the personal driver for the secretary of the United States Treasury, promised every indication of success. "You say they've become as thick as thieves?"

The driver drained his glass, turned toward the barman and raised his hand to solicit another. Banks always picked up the tab.

"Absolutely—the two of them meet every morning for coffee. But for the fact the secretary of state looks like the backend of bus, I would have said the minister has a crush on her."

"They must have important things of state to discuss," said Banks.

"Things of state my foot," scoffed the driver. I've heard several comments made by the general. He gets a little loud—at times, loud enough for me to hear what he's saying."

"What things? Do you think they're into each other," asked Banks.

"Nah. I probably shouldn't say this—while serving in the same administration, the general is extremely anti-Barrow. I wouldn't be surprised if the two of them are cooking up some sort of plot to have him impeached."

"Are you sure?" queried Banks.

"I'm positive something's up. The secretary has said several times how different she would do things if she were to be made president."

Banks called for another round of drinks. His friend's appetite for liquor made it easy for him to explore the possibilities of Eli Marion's concerns with regard to a conspiracy. Most politicians trusted their drivers and talked about business in front of them. It surprised him a U.S. secretary of the treasury could have an inroad to the coveted position of president. It did not, however, surprise Banks to find a military man involved in a conspiracy—an Air Force general. Both incumbents appeared to be over ambitious and it seemed unlikely they could make a coup happen. He painted all politicians and top-brass officials with the same brush—they all worked the system to serve themselves. The information came across to Banks as useful enough to share with Marion.

A short time later, armed with the accumulation of enough information to satisfy his client, Banks decided to call it a night and bid the driver goodbye. He left the pub and walked toward his car. The White House Chief of Staff would be eager to hear the news.

*

The president leaned back in his chair. "I would never have thought the secretary of the treasury would have the gumption for such a plan."

Marion sat opposite the presidential desk with his hands folded in his lap. With the media meeting behind them, the political atmosphere promised a more positive spin on the administration. After the brief all the journalists rushed back to their respective offices to tweak their stories.

"The involvement of two people who are far removed from the line of the presidency also surprised me until I did a little bit of investigation." said Marion. "The lines of succession to your position include designated survivors, who would be sworn in should a catastrophe strike congress and all the cabinet ministers are taken out in one foul swoop."

"Are you saying that one of these two people are a designated survivor?" Barrow asked.

"Not directly, Mr. President. Gary Chalmers, minister of Finance is to be the next one appointed. He will not be attending the next congressional meeting on Capitol Hill—however, guess who is to be designated should something happen to Chalmers before the meeting?"

"The secretary of the treasury?"

Marion's eyes gleamed. "Exactly. So, if they plan to initiate a takeover of the presidency, Chalmers's life is in great danger. I would think the only way for the secretary of the treasury to aspire to the throne is by eliminating her opposition, thus opening the door for her to be sworn in. After that we could expect a plot to bomb congress and kill off all the ministers, including yourself."

The president looked impressed. "Well done, Eli. I knew you would come up with the goods."

Marion chuckled. "And I didn't even have to play that part you said I was so good at."

"Point taken, Eli. Now, what are we going to do about these conspirators?"

"Leave it with me, Mr. President. I will take care of it. You will have your hands full—I've taken the liberty to arrange a meeting in the operations room. The joint chiefs and law enforcement heads will be here at 5:30 pm."

An aide knocked on the door and entered. "Excuse me, Mr. President but we have just received bad news about one of our cabinet ministers. Both Marion and the president froze.

"Who is it? Don't just stand there—tell us," the president commanded.

The young aide stammered out his news. "It's the minister of finance, sir—Mr. Chalmers. He was found murdered in his home about forty minutes ago."

The president and Marion stared at the aide and then at each other. "Oh my god. They moved on their part of the plan much quicker than I anticipated," said Marion.

"If only your source came up with the information sooner," said the president. "We might have been able to protect the minister."

"You mean I should have considered the implications sooner and we might have been able to prevent it," said Marion.

"Don't blame yourself, Eli. It is what it is. At least we know what the next part of the plan is.

*

Minutes after the release of the 6:00 pm news, the denizens of every large city in the country voiced their fear of a nuclear calamity and people started to evacuate to country areas. It happened at the appropriate times as per time zone. People not yet ready to flee gathered outside local government buildings and demonstrated their concerns. Others in lessor populated cities and smaller towns were calmer but these remained in a state of apprehension.

All banks and financial subsidiaries shut their doors. Grocery chains soon ran out of food. Ten minutes before the news hit the streets, the president issued an executive order for martial law and, as if the state of affairs appeared not dire enough, the entire rail network in the country shutdown. The Pentagon computers suffered several virus attacks, which threw the military into a state of confusion and left little doubt of Merlin's active interference in national systems. The bureaucrats of Washington DC subsided into a huddle of headhunters, each in an attempt to think of potential solutions. They fixed blame to anyone from the previous administrations who still carried a position in the present government.

President Barrow, Eli Marion, the heads of law enforcement and the Joint Chiefs, locked themselves into the operations room. No one would be allowed home until Merlin's location could be established. If a ballistic missile hit any of the cities the president would be evacuated to the bunker in Cheyenne. Some deemed it more secure for him to use Air Force One and rule the country from the air.

Barrow looked around at all the familiar faces. "What can you report regarding the sea search for the Taft?"

The Chief of the Navy stood to his feet. "We have the Universal Conquest, out largest carrier out in the Pacific—its air compliment is sweeping large parts of the ocean. We have F/A-18's in the air, accompanied by SH-60-R's and S-3B Vikings, the best sub hunters in the world. It will only be a matter of time, Mr. President."

"Let's hope we still have time, General. I have some more important news. Tomorrow congress was to convene at Capitol Hill but we have reason to believe foul play is expected. I have instructed the secretary to cancel the meeting and reconvene it in forty-eight hours. Everyone will be informed. Eli has contacted the FBI with regards to two individuals who we believe are involved in a conspiracy to hijack the presidency."

The president explained how the sudden death of the finance minister, the congress meetings appointed designated survivor, made way for a certain cabinet minister to be sworn in.

James Ingram, the deputy head of the FBI, asked to be heard. The president motioned him to speak.

"We have already picked up the persons involved in this conspiracy. They are not saying anything and we don't know, at this point, if anyone else is involved. It is, therefore a good thing that congress is delayed until we can assure someone else is not going to detonate a bomb and kill off the cabinet. Capitol Hill is being thoroughly searched for explosive devices."

"Good work, James. What news about the search for Merlin's lair?"

"We are working on it, Mr. President. My men are closing in and it will only be a matter of time. They have found the original workshop Jones used to build his super computer and from where much of the harassment was broadcasted. Jones has moved the lair to a new place. Special Agent O'-Malley has requested a bomb squad to visit the venue—I have not heard anything consequently. "

"Unfortunately time is something which is not on our side, James, however, we understand this is a difficult task. Keep us updated."

James Ingram's cell phone rang and he grabbed it out of his pocket. "Excuse me, Mr. President. I think this might be the call I've been waiting for."

The room went silent as everyone waited for the assistant director to complete the call. When finished he replaced the phone in his pocket and stared around at everyone. His face appeared pale.

"We have just received news of an explosion in Queens, New York early this morning. It was the building my men were investigating."

∞∞

22

Trouble for the Team

Dr. Jones' words reverberated off the inner walls of the premises. The team of FBI agents stared in horror at the speaker mounted above the door which lead outside to the business frontage. Jones' message contained some irony.

"Your efforts so far have been remarkable, Special Agent O'Malley, but even the great FBI cannot defeat my plan. The USS Taft is almost in position for the release of its payload and soon the United States Government will rue the day they crossed swords with Merlin Jones."

O'Malley shouted at the speaker, his voice filled with venom. "You won't get away with this, Jones. You're going to murder millions of people in an effort to gain revenge for the accidental killing of three family members—your idea of fair retribution is way out of proportion."

His words echoed throughout the corridor but could not be heard by the infamous genius. Jones' intention never included a two-way conversation between himself and the captives. His voice cut across O'Malley's tirade.

"In few moments you will know your destiny. I have rigged the building with enough explosive to level it completely. You will find the outside doors will have all locked electronically but being the benevolent person I am, I will give you a few minutes to consider your part in the killing of my family members."

"Jones—don't do this," shouted O'Malley.

*

Merlin Jones gazed at the screen, which displayed the images of the four FBI agents, in the doomed building. He could see the words formed by O'Malley's lips but could not hear them.

"How far is the Taft from the designated position, Merlin?"

"It has one hundred nautical miles to go, Dr. Jones."

"Are there any factors that might complicate the final step?"

"Not really, Dr. Jones. The Admiral Kalnikov is trailing the sub by several miles and poses a danger, however, I have a plan and am convinced nothing will be able to stop us."

"What is the state of the country?"

"The whole nation is in an uproar and a fortuitous move by two ambitious politicians has played right into our hands. I have hacked the president's personal mail and it appears there is an attempt being made at a coup. The president has just declared martial law throughout the nation and the fabric of the society is in a slow collapse."

"Excellent, Merlin. You have done absolute wonders."

"The credit belongs to you, Dr. Jones—you are my creator."

*

A flash of light dazzled O'Malley's eyes. "So this is how it all ends?" he mumbled to no one in particular. The corridor dissolved into white light and his colleagues disappeared before his eyes, yet he felt no sensation of pain or concussion. With a jolt he came to consciousness in a familiar place, but couldn't put his finger on his surroundings or the sudden experience. O'Malley floated along in a semi-darkness for several seconds before the scene triggered his memory—the inside of someone's brain. He recognized the flashes of color and the presence of neurons, with the familiar dendrites, axons and fluid, which transported his avatar along a lengthy conduit. A flashback to his previous case: the Memory Sweep.

Dr. Lucas Wheeler and Samantha Pink, the inventors of the Nobel prize-winning Memory Sweeper, which the FBI used to find the conspirators of President Martin Lewis's assassination, came to mind. O'Malley's journey into the mind of the assassin, Robert Coulson, appeared to re-occur through an entangled, quantum state and manifest itself in a former memory. The strange phenomenon happened several times after the initial experiment, with one caveat: on each previous occasion he saw Coulson mouth a word, which appeared to be, "flower."

This time the vision appeared with a difference. He saw Coulson point to a steel trapdoor in a concrete floor. What could it mean? The transfer of information appeared to take place at times of extreme stress—was it useful information or the figment of an overwrought imagination?

The white light which surrounded his position began to dissipate and with a gradual clarity, his three friends appeared out of the gloom. Gabby held onto him from behind, with both her arms while Martinez and MacDonald made an attempt to revive him from his stupor.

"Boss, boss—can you hear me," shouted Mac-Donald. Martinez ran down the corridor to the main workshop and searched the high, barred windows for a place to get out of the building. He jumped up onto one of the workbenches and smashed the glass window but thick, steel bars prevented any progress. O'Malley shook his head, opened his eyes wide and turned to MacDonald.

"Look for a steel trapdoor in the floor. I have just seen one in a flashback," said O'Malley.

"A flashback?" MacDonald queried.

Gabby supplied a quick explanation. "He's been having these visions ever since the episode with the memory sweeper experience.

MacDonald jumped up, released O'Malley and shouted to Martinez. "Diego—look for a trapdoor in the floor."

Martinez went silent for a minute while he pointed his flashlight over sections of the floor in the workshop.

"I see it," he shouted. "Help me move this workbench—its underneath."

The two men combined their strength to shove the heavy bench aside to give access to the steel trapdoor. Gabby helped O'Malley to his feet and the two of them stumbled forward, toward the main workshop, in the murky, morning light.

"Quick. Get in here. It appears to be an underground tunnel but I have no idea where it goes," said MacDonald.

O'Malley thrust Gabby toward the trapdoor and cast a glance over his shoulder. "It doesn't matter. The floor is thick, reinforced concrete and should protect us from the explosives. The blast will more than likely be deflected upward and that will lessen the impact on us," he said.

They scrambled down the ladder provided to find themselves in a reinforced basement about twenty feet square. MacDonald slammed the trapdoor shut seconds before a tremendous explosion shook the entire building. Dust from two steel beams, which served as extra supports, rained down on them and they flattened their bodies onto the basement's floor. O'Malley stretched himself over Gabby who wound her arms around his neck. Their ears rang with the concussion of the blast and for a moment, all the air seemed to be sucked out of the small room. Outside, pieces of roof construction cascaded down on the plot and a plume of smoke reached high up into the sky.

The four agents struggled to breathe as the explosion sucked out all the available oxygen in the space. In the aftermath, fumes from the blast permeated through the trapdoor, to fill the basement and they lost consciousness.

*

The lieutenant, a tactical bomb technician and expert in bomb disposal attached to the NYPD bomb squad, received the call from O'Malley at approximately 6:10 am. He gathered his team and they raced over to Queens as fast as their van could travel. They heard the explosion and saw the plume of smoke while still on approach to the address and their hearts fell. This would no longer be defuse and disposal, but a recovery operation. They arrived outside the premises to see the building destroyed. Several small fires raged at ground zero.

The lieutenant issued a terse order to his two companion technicians. "We're too late. The FBI agent told me they were inside the building so I don't give much for their chances of survival. Search for any signs of remains."

They clambered out of the van and raced toward the site. No one bothered with the usual bomb protection gear. When the intensity of the fires diminished the squad moved in for a quick inspection of the damage. Each carried a long steel prod with which they could move hot debris, in the search for survivors. The floor of the demolished building lay thick with rubble and it became difficult to see the parameters of the original rooms. One of the technicians brought several plastic recovery bags in the event they found any human remains. The men turned over lumps of concrete and raked out large items of debris for about five minutes, until the lieutenant called a short break.

"Not a sign of any human remains so far. I wonder if they managed to escape."

"If they did they would have surely waited for us to arrive—we were just around the corner when the blast went off."

"You have a point. Start to clear the floor of as much debris as you can. We need to see if there aren't any possible underground storage bays."

They rested for another five minutes and then started to sweep the floors of the various rooms. The lieutenant spoke to a few of the bystanders from other businesses in the area, but no one saw anything of significance, accept for one person who saw a vehicle pull up as he drove by to turn in next door, minutes before the explosion. He pointed to MacDonald's SUV, parked fifty yards away. After a quick inspection of the vehicle the lieutenant concluded the FBI agents might still be somewhere in the vicinity. One of the bomb techs called to him.

"I think I've found something, Lieutenant."

He jogged back to the site and stared at the space on the ground, to which the tech pointed. It looked like a trapdoor. "Open it, but be careful—there may be a fire in the hole."

Both the techs pulled on the ring attached to the door and opened it with care. Fumes billowed out and the lieutenant knelt down to peer inside. He shouted and jumped into the chamber. "Quick, help me—there are people down here."

The other two sprang into action and followed him into the basement. Four bodies lay huddled together, their faces covered with their hands but none of them appeared to be alive. "We must get them out of here and apply CPR."

One of the techs climbed back up the ladder and positioned himself at the trapdoor entrance while the other two lifted the inert bodies of the FBI agents and hauled them out of the basement. They were laid down on the grass lawn of the business frontage and the techs, all trained in CPR, went to work. By this time, a large group of by-standers had gathered to watch the proceedings. In the distance a siren wailed, an indication of the lieutenant's hasty call for medical help. One of the people in the crowd, a young woman, raced up to where they worked. "I'm a trained nurse; I can help with CPR."

Two more people, trained in first aid, joined them and they persevered until one of them shout-ed, "This one's breathing."

O'Malley lifted his head and stared around, at the gathered crowd.

Minutes later, Martinez came around and so did MacDonald. O'Malley raised himself onto an elbow and watched the nurse work on Gabby. The lieutenant took over from the nurse after she ran out of steam, but could not get a response from the victim. He worked harder and kept mumbling, "Come on, girl—wake up."

O'Malley recalled the encounter he and Gabby enjoyed while in his apartment. With a sudden rush of emotion he realized he could not bear to lose her. In a moment of panic he considered a di-vorce from Janet to marry Gabby, should she live. The lieutenant stopped his efforts and turned to O'Malley.

"She's gone, sir—there is no response."

O'Malley looked with despair at MacDonald and Martinez. Martinez rushed forward, pushed the lieutenant aside and threw himself on Gabby's body. "No—no," he shouted. "God, don't let her die."

∞∞

23

The Kalnikov and the Taft face off.

The driving wind launched the spray high over the Taft's sail as its hull broke the surface. Commander Bill Lowell gained a measure of solace in the possibility of the sub being blown out of the water. Their lives would end but so would the threat to millions of his countrymen, women and children. The sea raged around the submarine as it rolled with the swells and on occasion, the sail appeared to disappear from the destroyer's view. The Taft's sonar consoles with their sonic enhancements, showed the destroyer to be at a distance of one thousand yards.

The submarine maintained its position on the surface, with the upper part of the hull and the sail presenting an intermittent visibility. Lowell kept his eyes on the weapon's fire control instrumentation and spawned a theory: a torpedo fired from the stern tubes at one thousand yards would provide a difficult scenario for the destroyer's captain.

A sudden jolt surged through the Taft and the sub altered its course by a few degrees. The Kalnikov's first salvo fell twenty feet off the submarine's port bow.

*

Captain Rodin couldn't believe his eyes. The surfaced submarine, within a stone's throw of the destroyer, heralded a wonderful opportunity for him to use his six-inch cannons.

"Turret B—fire as soon as you can line up on that sail."

A second later the boom of the six inch gun could be heard above the wail of the wind. The Taft rolled in the troughs as the first salvo fell within six yards of her port beam.

"Keep firing until you hit it," shouted Rodin.

The turret operator grunted an acknowledgment as he continued to attempt a direct lineup with the sail. The constant buck-and-heave of the ship in the heavy sea hindered accurate marksmanship. His second shot ranged ahead of the sub's starboard bow, evident by a huge plume of spray at the spot where the shell landed. The sub altered course by a few degrees and the gunner took up a new aim. The ship's executive officer stood rigid at the windshield with his binoculars trained on the rear of the Taft.

"Captain—the submarine has fired a torpedo from one of its stern tubes. It will be running in about twenty foot of water."

"Time remaining to impact?" Rodin asked.

"Approximately thirty-five seconds, Captain."

Rodin called to the engine room to reduce speed and at the same time commanded the helmsman to swing twenty degrees to starboard. The Kalnikov reacted with swift precision to the captain's instruction and they watched the sonar screen as the torpedo raced toward them at a speed of fifty knots.

"Release counter measures," shouted Rodin.

"Counter measures released, sir. The torpedo is being distracted."

"It will miss us by a small margin," shouted the executive officer.

"Fifteen degrees to port, for five seconds—then dead ahead," called Rodin.

Fortunately for the Russian destroyer's crew, the Kalnikov had the very latest Bell Crown intercept decoy system at their disposal, which made the Taft's Black shark and Mark 48 torpedoes vulnerable to diversion.

The Kalnikov swung back in a short arc toward its original direction as the run of the sea hit them head on. The ship breached a huge wave, charged down the other side of the swell and lost sight of the sub's sail. A moment later they breasted another swell to see the Taft dead ahead of them. The Taft appeared to wallow in the waves. He raised his glasses and caught a view of the stationary hull, which presented an occasional exposure, due the wash of the heavy sea.

"Pick up your fire again," he shouted.

The gunners in "B" turret started up with two more salvos but the shells flew well ahead of the sub and their combined splashes rose high into the air.

"Sorry, Captain. The manual adjustments are not as quick as the computer guided siting system. It would appear the gun's manual site parameters need an adjustment. We are over-shooting the target," said the chief gunner of the turret.

"I will have you up on orders, Marin. The program that runs your sights should have been checked long before this, now get it right. Switch to computer assisted sighting, immediately. "

The gunner's voice sounded hoarse. "The technician is working on the manual adjustment system. I have already tried computer assisted guidance but it just goes crazy, sir."

Rodin turned to his XO. "That supercomputer on the Taft is still messing with our equipment."

He called on the fire control officer. "Vladimir —release torpedoes immediately."

The fire control officer sounded apologetic. "Sorry, Captain. The torpedo fire control system cannot be accessed manually like the others. We need to switch back to the master computer, otherwise the system will remain locked."

Rodin cursed. In his moment of need the world conspired against him. The Taft's abductor was out maneuvering him at every turn. He knew the Kalnikov's two main anti-sub deterrents, torpedoes and rockets, required the fire control's computer to function but he had not anticipated the Taft making a defense from the surface.

The executive officer tried to keep his voice calm. "Captain—two torpedoes approaching."

"Release counter measures," said the Captain.

"Released, sir—no—something has malfunctioned. I'm trying to free up the deployment system."

"Hurry," shouted Rodin. "Those torpedoes will be on us in less than half a minute."

The men on the bridge waited for confirmation of the counter measure to come but it never did. Instead, a huge vibration accompanied by a roar of sound, emanated throughout the Kalnikov as the two torpedoes struck the warship, one on the starboard side of the bow and the other near the stern.

"We have taken two hits, Captain," shouted the executive officer.

Rodin went cold. "Give me a damage report. I need to know if we are taking on water. Is that confounded sight on the cannon working yet?"

"We need a few more minutes, sir," shouted the chief gunner.

"We don't have any more time, Marin. I am turning the vessel to give 'A' turret a line to the submarine."

The Kalnikov needed to cut across the stern of the sub in order to give the other turret a better view. He gave the appropriate order and the ship began to turn with short sluggish moves.

"The steering has been affected by one of the torpedoes, Captain," said the executive officer."

For the first time in his life, Rodin contemplated death as a reality. To have suffered the first hit in a tactical battle scared him and rocked his confidence. If the adjacent turret could not be brought to bear, all would be lost.

"Can they fix the steering?" he asked.

The executive officer replied. "I can't raise the engine room, sir. Maybe they are suffering a loss of electrical power to their communications. I will go and see."

He clutched at whatever supports could be found in the headlong flight down the stairway, to the corridor below. The Kalnikov wallowed in the trough of two mighty waves and for several seconds the men on the bridge shouted out in fear as it appeared the ship might capsize. The slow turn by the destroyer, to bring the adjacent turret to bear on the Taft, took interminable seconds of valuable time. The sub lay dead ahead.

Rodin shouted at the turret's chief gunner. "I have given you a better look, Alexei. Make sure you hit the submarine with all that can be thrown at it."

"The sail is lined up, Captain, firing the first salvo," cried the gunner.

The destroyer bucked under the shock as the six-inch weapon released its projectile of death. Rodin looked and could no longer see the sail in the boiling froth of water.

"They are diving, Alexei—keep on firing. We can't allow them to escape."

Several more shells whistled toward their targets, which caused the surface of the sea in the sub's last known position, to boil with froth and plumes of spray. The executive officer returned, his face pale. Perspiration coursed down his flushed cheeks and panic registered in his eyes.

"The engine room is flooded, Captain. The engineers are all dead and in minutes, we are going to be dead in the water."

To support the executive officer's bad news, the Kalnikov slowed and came to stop. Rodin experienced a sudden, intense fear. Another explosion rocked the vessel as the Taft's final torpedo, fired seconds before the dive, slammed into the port bow of the destroyer. The Kalnikov listed on the port side and the men hung onto the bridge's main console for dear life.

The captain's fear dissipated as his training kicked in. He understood what needed to be done.

"Radio operator—send out a transmission to the helicopter and tell them they cannot return to us. Also contact the naval base at Rybachiy and send them our position—inform them we are abandoning ship."

*

Bill Lowell watched the sonar consoles. The enhancements which represented the Kalnikov, indicated the destroyer to have stopped all forward motion. The loudness of the signal began to diminish as the sub slipped deeper into the dark ocean and started to pull away. Merlin's tactics still seemed an enigma to the commander but the AI's victory impressed him. He considered the fate of the destroyer's crew. A sensation of relief, accompanied by sadness and dread, coursed through his being. The sub's survival meant he and his crew would still live for an undetermined period.

The Taft, however, would soon reach the optimal position for a preemptive strike on United States cities. Lowell glanced at his watch. The opportunity to sabotage one of the forward torpedoes still remained a possibility. The shift's maintenance team made ready to move in and perform the sabotage mission, allocated to them. Lowell left the control room in search of Chief Petty Officer Hunt.

The commander found his man in the wardroom where they took their usual corner table. The two men sat and stared at each other for several seconds before Lowell spoke.

"Are your men ready to take on the final attempt at sinking the Taft?" The Commander whispered.

"We are ready, sir. Nobody feels there is still reason to hope we will survive. The torpedo room is now pumped dry—there is nothing more to be said."

"The AI has proved it is capable of carrying out its mission. The Kalnikov appears to be dead in the water so it no longer poses a threat. We are the last resort, unless the sub is picked up by aircraft when it comes near to the surface to fire the missiles. The existing weather will make it extremely difficult."

"Do you think the Kalnikov sank?" Hunt asked.

"I don't know. We recorded several hits by the Taft's rear-tube torpedoes. It's a tragedy but the destroyer no longer features in our hope of receiving some justice. You must tell your men we have to do everything required to succeed in the sabotage attempt."

"They are ready to give their lives—they understand the odds are totally against us."

Lowell understood the petty officer's sentiments. "The point, though, is we have an opportunity to save the lives of millions of Americans."

Hunt glanced at the clock above the entrance to the wardroom. "Two hours to go. Let's hope Merlin doesn't have his suspicions raised by our actions. Any human being would know the crew's position is hopeless and the men would not bother to perform routine maintenance under these circumstances."

*

Captain Rodin checked through the crew quarters and ship's galley to satisfy himself no members still remained on the ship. Apart from the dead men in the engine room everyone appeared to have found a place in one of the several life-vessels, four of which already floated in the heavy sea. His own emergency vessel awaited his patronage and he took one last look around the ship's bridge. The memories flowed and tears welled up in his eyes. There would be no order of bravery for him.

The ship now listed at a thirty degree angle in the tumultuous waters of the sea and the gunnel dipped under the heaving surface of the waves. Rodin stepped off the bridge and made his way to the emergency vessel, which still hung on its davit about six feet above the water. The executive officer beckoned to him.

"Come, Captain—leave her to her destiny. She has fought the good fight and there is nothing more to be done."

With the XO's help he leapt across the gap and disappeared into the innards of the lifeboat. Minutes later, the Kalnikov slipped below the waves and descended to its watery grave.

∞∞

24

About that Flashback.

O'Malley pulled Martinez off Gabby's prone body. The Hispanic struggled to get loose from his grip as the lieutenant stepped in to help. You can't do anything for her, Diego," said O'Malley

"Leave me alone," shouted Martinez. The distraught agent tore away from O'Malley moments before the unexpected happened. A sudden cough and a splutter accompanied by a substantial amount of frothy spittle exuded from Gabby's lips.

"She's still alive," shouted MacDonald.

The lieutenant turned and dropped to his knees and placed his hand behind the hapless agent's head to lift her neck and free the trachea. A volume of spume-like liquid bubbled out of her mouth as he turned the head sideways. Both O'Malley and Martinez stared with wide open eyes.

"Give me a hand to turn her over," said the lieutenant. MacDonald helped him roll Gabby onto her stomach. She spluttered before glazed eyes opened to stare at the ground. The lieutenant waited a few minutes and then with MacDonald's help, turned her over onto her back again.

"Bring us some water," he shouted. One of the bomb disposal techs came forward with a water bottle and they poured water onto Gabby's parched lips. O'Malley knelt down and placed his hand behind her head.

"Welcome back, Gabriella. You gave us all a nasty scare."

Gabby smiled at O'Malley. "It takes more than a little explosion and some smoke to keep me down, boss."

"I see that," he said. "I don't know what I would do if I lost you." He knew the words carried a hint of his feelings but for O'Malley, the time had come. His life could not continue in the same direction anymore. He needed an anchor for his soul, a relationship that didn't submit him to continual judgment, or demand he forget about the past. He bent his neck and kissed Gabby's dry lips.

"I love you, Gabs."

She looked at him in adoration and lifted her hand to grab his shirt. "I'll hold you to that, Dillon. I've always loved you."

Martinez stared at the couple with a growing sense of realization. The notion that Gabby might be in love with her boss never occurred to him. A sadness swept over his heart to be replaced by a hollow feeling of loss, but he held no grudges. In the astuteness of his street-wise philosophy— sometime you won and sometimes you lost.

The siren in the remote distance grew in typical Doppler style until, with a screech of tires, an emergency vehicle pulled up to the sidewalk in front of the decimated building. Two paramedics jumped out, each with a bag of medical supplies and instruments. O'Malley moved to one side for them to inspect Gabby.

MacDonald flashed his badge. "Give her a thorough inspection—she's been the victim of smoke inhalation."

Gabby tried to stand. "I'm fine, Roland—I don't need doctoring."

She collapsed in the process and tried again but the paramedics restrained her.

"Let them do their job, Gabriella," said O'Malley.

*

Gabby and O'Malley sat together on the bench in the FBI staff clinic. A few moments later a doctor walked in and smiled at them.

"In the wars again, Special Agent O'Malley?'

O'Malley chuckled. "You could call it that, doc. It's not me I'm worried about but Gabriella here." He pointed to Gabby.

She shook her head. "There's nothing wrong with me, I swear, doc. Just a bit of smoke inhalation but I'm fine now."

"Let me be the judge of that." the doctor looked into her eyes with his ophthalmoscope. Satisfied at what he saw he lifted the stethoscope, listened to her heart and checked her pulse rate.

"I told you so," she said.

"You're as healthy as a horse but you are showing signs of strain—you need rest."

"I'll be sure to get plenty of that, doc," she said. O'Malley rolled his eyes.

The doctor laughed. "Don't worry, Dillon. I know she doesn't listen to anybody."

"Can we go now?" Gabby asked.

"You are free to go, but please take my suggestion of rest seriously."

They walked back down the corridor to the elevator, which led up to the investigation department offices. Their arms touched and Gabby's fingers entwined with his. He turned his head to look at her and she smiled. He wanted to kiss her right there but the elevator bell dinged, the doors opened and disgorged a group of people.

She whispered in his ear. "What about us, Dillon? When are we going to take some time to talk about our future?"

O'Malley glanced at her and said, "It will have to wait, Gabs. You know how I feel about you but time is of the essence. We have a job to do. When this is all over we'll sit down and talk."

She smiled and leaned her head on his shoulder.

*

Gabby, MacDonald and Martinez sat around O'Malley's desk and listened as the special agent described his strange experience. "It's happened a few times before—a sort of flashback I have been having. This last time, however, it was different—I clearly saw President Lewis's killer, Robert Coulson, point at a trapdoor in the floor. I knew instinctively it had to be within the building."

MacDonald leaned back in his chair. "Do you think the flashbacks might be related to your last case—the one with the memory sweep?"

Yes, I think it might be. You all know I lead the investigation on the assassination conspiracy, which led to Coulson's arrest and eventual exposure of the conspirators. Ever since that time I've had several of these experiences, all focused on the same scene. I see Coulson look at me and mouth a word. I am not a great lip-reader but it seemed to be the word: 'flower'. Can't make head or tail of it."

Martinez, always the smart one, came up with a solution. "You need to make contact with that Professor What's-his-name?"

"Professor Wheeler of the Neuroscience Institute?"

"Yeah," retorted Martinez. "You should go and see him. From what I remember you guys delved deeply into this Coulson guy's shit. I don't quite understand the quantum physics thing, but I think you might still have some sort of contact with this dude's mind."

A light went on in O'Malley's head. "I think you've hit the nail on the head, Diego. You're one smart guy, you know that?"

"Yeah, sure boss, I know that but certain other people think I'm a moron."

Gabby rolled her eyes, got up and slapped Martinez on the shoulder. "Come off it, Diego. I apologized for calling you that—let it go now."

Martinez ducked another shoulder slap and caught her wrist but let it go when she glared at him.

"That's exactly what I'm going to do—go see the professor," said O'Malley.

He removed Wheeler's card from his wallet and placed the call. After a brief conversation he turned to the others. "The professor wants me to pay him a visit. I'm going there right now."

Gabby jumped up. "I'm not letting you out of my sight, Dillon. I'm coming with you."

Martinez and MacDonald glanced at each other. "I guess we'll just get onto researching companies and what purchases and other expenditures they have. Before Merlin's latest escapade hit the fan, we were busy narrowing down a list of potential suspects in the New York Metropolitan area," said MacDonald. The two agents left the briefing room.

O'Malley stood to his feet. "Let's go. You drive, Gabs."

Fifteen minutes later they walked into the Institute and were greeted by the dean. O'Malley introduced Gabby and asked for Professor Wheeler. "You'll find him and Sam working on something in the laboratory."

"I know my way," said O'Malley.

On the way to the lab O'Malley briefed Gabby on professor Wheeler's secretary, Samantha. "She's real quirky, trendy, outspoken, funky and brilliant."

"And what part did she play in your life, Dillon?"

"Not my type. However, don't judge the book by its cover—she's plenty smart."

"And probably annoying, like Martinez."

"She grows on people. Give her a chance—I feel you've already prejudged her," said O'Malley.

Gabby's lip's tightened to a mere slit and she dropped behind O'Malley, to follow in his wake. They rounded a corner in the corridor and entered the lab. The smell of chemicals filled the air and brought back some memories, to stir O'Malley's sensibilities.

"Dillon. Good to see you, chum. Where have you been hiding?"

"Oh, here and there, Lucas," said O'Malley in modesty. "A little run-in with a supercomputer, is all."

Samantha ran to O'Malley, threw her arms around his neck and planted a kiss on his lips. Taken a little aback he held her at arm's length. "Sam, you're looking as funky as ever."

"Not as good as you do, sweetie."

He introduced Gabby to them, who forced a smile.

He couldn't help see Gabby's reaction to Samantha's greeting. Her face looked like thunder but she held her peace.

Lucas Wheeler clasped O'Malley's hand and pumped it up and down in delight. "Let's go to my office and talk."

They walked to his office and parked themselves on chairs while the professor sat behind his desk. "Now what's this about flashbacks?"

O'Malley told them about the recurring experience. "They started to happen recently, after I started on my latest case. I won't say Robert Coulson has suddenly become my hero but something he revealed to me in this most recent flashback, actually saved our lives."

Sam took over. "This is one of those after effects we are concerned about. There is so much we don't yet understand about particle physics and the quantum realm. I feel it's quite plausible though that you have retained a certain amount of entanglement with Coulson's mind. The effect could be a draw back of your right brain consciousness to his memory, when you are under stress."

"There's been plenty of that recently," said Gabby.

"The papers are full of the bank fiasco and a disruption on Wall Street. I guess this latest revelation has to do with the case you are on," said the professor.

"There's more to it but its classified and I can't talk about it," answered O'Malley.

Further discussion with regard to the possible quantum effects on the human mind followed and one sure point came out of it.

"You need to pay Coulson a prison visit. Your mind is consciously searching for an answer to a stressful problem—through the entanglement process you and Coulson appear to share occasional particle contact. There is something he might be able to help you with," said Wheeler.

"I guess you're right, Lucas. I'll make the necessary arrangements," said O'Malley.

They parted company with the promise of a future get-together for drinks and the two agents climbed into the Chevy, for the return to FBI headquarters.

Gabby spoke first. "That woman has certainly got your number, Dillon."

"Take no notice of her, Gabs. I doubt she knows what she wants."

"She wants you, buster."

"Nah. You don't know her. She actually has the hots for the professor, but he's all work."

"I can tell she's in love with you, Dillon."

The comment irritated O'Malley. "Let's just drop it okay, Gabriella."

"I rest my case," she said.

"Women," he mused.

Back at the office O'Malley placed a call to the maximum security prison authority in Otisville, New York. The warden granted him an immediate audience with Coulson.

"I'm coming with you, Dillon," said Gabby.

"Let's get going, then," said O'Malley. "As I said before, time is of the essence."

∞∞

25

The Taft gets into Position.

The USS William Taft pierced the dark, depths of the North Pacific waters like a ghost. Despite the fleets of U.S., Russian, British and Chinese submarines in a structured pattern of surveillance, no trace of the Taft's passage could be detected. The hunters clung to a truth—the renegade lurked somewhere in the Pacific Ocean, a large volume of water, to conduct a search in.

At 2300 hours the sonar supervisor made a comment. "Contact bearing 137, at thirty-five kilometers, Commander."

Lowell glanced at Hunt and they moved closer to the bank of sonar consoles, to observe the enhancements on the screens. The faint rectangular images registered for a moment and then changed color.

"Merlin has switched to stealth mode again," said the operator. "If it's a navy vessel I think it might have picked us up."

Lowell raised his eyebrows. "I'm pretty sure most of the great powers have their navies on the lookout for us. There could be dozens of vessels involved."

"It appears to be keeping a constant distance from us," said Hunt.

"I will let you know as soon as I detect the blade rate," said the sonar supervisor.

The navigator chipped in. "I think we might be getting near the optimum firing position, for the ballistic missiles, sir."

"What do your calculations show, Nav?"

"For the missiles to travel a distance of under four thousand miles, which is their established maximum range, the sub would need to come within one thousand miles of the coast. The optimum distance would be one of several latitude points and about one thousand miles off the West coast of the United States."

"You are saying that Merlin will choose a position from where all major cities can be targeted, thereby releasing the payload from one position?"

"That is my prognosis, sir. I figured this would pose the least risk of discovery. You can be assured that the AI realizes the ability of the searchers to work out such a position and wait around for the Taft to turn up. I would think the sub will rise quickly in one spot and release the payload consecutively until they have all been deployed. Once this has been accomplished there will be no further use for the Taft and the AI will simply allow it to be destroyed."

"Where exactly do you think this firing position will be?" Lowell asked.

"Right here, sir." The navigator placed his finger on the navigation chart.

"That's about one thousand nautical miles off the Baja."

"That is correct, Commander. A vessel situated in this spot could fire off its missile payload and hit any city, between Los Angeles and New York."

Lowell stared at the map. "We are only about sixty miles from that point. At a speed of forty miles per hour we will be there in about one hour and twenty-eight minutes."

Hunt caught the commander's eye and they both nodded. There remained enough time for the accomplishment of their mission in the torpedo room.

Lowell glanced at his watch. "I'll see you in the wardroom in forty-five minutes. Prepare your men."

Hunt acknowledged the instruction and left the control room. The commander turned to the sonar supervisor. "Keep me informed regarding any change in that distant vessel's position."

The commander's stateroom suffered the same almost unbreathable atmosphere as the rest of the sub. Lowell collapsed onto this bunk in exhaustion and stared at the family photo, which rested on the adjacent desk.

*

Certain members of the crew, chosen for the special mission waited with bated breath, for the hour of midnight. At 2400 hours, as per standard procedure, a crew of cleaners and an engineer moved into the torpedo room, to perform regular maintenance. The engineer, armed with jumper cables and tools hidden in a mobile janitor bucket with its mop, took up position adjacent to the battery inspection plate of their target torpedo. The others took up various positions where they could fake the cleaning of tubes and cable racks. One of the men stationed himself with the mop in line with the single camera to obstruct Merlin's view of the proceedings.

The men made a pact to stay in the room while the process took its course. The entrance door could be locked from inside the torpedo room. This would be their final opportunity. Merlin maintained a rigorous watch on all the systems. They did not want to alert the AI to their mission. The breathable atmosphere in the sub still brought a tremendous discomfort to the men but they all resigned themselves to be the cause of the Taft's final demise.

*

Chief Petty Officer Hunt lay on the bunk in his cramped sleeping quarters and held the junior officer's gaze. She looked at him with intent and a glimmer of a smile crossed her lips. A chance meeting at a Christmas Navy Ball several months prior, due to strict navy regulations, started them on a guarded relationship. The discovery that they would be colleagues on the same vessel complicated the matter further, but neither gave up.

Sandra Hart had taken an instant interest in the tall, handsome young officer with his short cropped blond hair and athletic body. They both knew their bond of friendship would soon change into a full-blown love affair should their work commitments allow it. The four-month stint to date included an occasional meal in the galley together and clandestine glances at each other whenever the opportunity arose. The status quo, however, changed at the point of the Taft's abduction by the AI. Since that time, they met in secluded alcoves and off-limit rooms careful to not attract any attention to themselves, in a pretense they were just friends.

Hunt coughed and wiped his mouth with a handkerchief. The air smelled stale and old. They wouldn't last another twenty-four hours in his estimation, unless the AI decided otherwise. The premise of twenty-four hours sounded on the positive side as the Taft would not survive the intended sabotage, which was due to take place within an hour. Hunt and Hart decided to speed up their relationship.

"I don't give a shit who sees us now. All I want to do is make love to you and when the sabotage mission is complete, we can die in each other's arms." He pulled on the curtain and closed off the bunk.

Tears started to flow down Sandra's cheeks and she reached out to him with both arms. "I have loved you from the moment we first met," she said. "Unfortunately work regulations have messed up any chance of a normal relationship."

He held her to his bosom. "We have little time left so we should make the most of it."

He slid his hand beneath the open front of her coverall and rubbed her one breast softly. Their lips met in a passionate clash of sensuality followed by a hasty divestment of clothes. Soon they lay naked on the bunk with a mutual resolve—to make the most of their short time together. Everyone else would be occupied and Hunt did not expect any interruptions. The time slipped by with silent unobtrusiveness and a sudden sound of footsteps heralded the end to their first and only attempt to do what couples in love did under normal circumstances.

A sailor stopped next to the bunk and called his name. "Chief—sorry to interrupt but you are due to meet with Commander Lowell in five minutes."

Hunt acknowledged the call and told the sailor he would be out in a few minutes. He looked into Sandra's eyes and saw the emotional pain. He kissed her and said, "I love you, Sandie. You know what is about to happen and it's important you wait here for me. Once I've seen the maintenance crew off to their task, I will return. We will face the end together."

The tears streamed down her cheeks as she reached out with one hand and touched his face. She flung her arms around his neck. "I will love you forever."

He held her in his arms for a long moment. It took all his courage to release her and slip through the curtain to step onto the hard floor of the sleeping quarters. He donned his coverall and walked off to the wardroom, where the commander awaited him.

*

A voice called through the intercom but it took several attempts before Lowell surfaced from his memories. His first recollections were confused and then the awful truth hit him. They would soon be dead.

"Commander to the bridge."

He rolled off the bunk and pulled on his boots. The foul air stuck in his lungs and for several seconds he coughed violently. After clearing his throat Lowell opened the stateroom door and headed for the bridge. The men coughed incessantly into the palms of their hands and the heads of several young sailors, nodded back and forth with exhaustion.

The sonar supervisor caught his eye. "There are twelve more vessels that have joined in the search, sir. I think they are all submarines—none of them have made up any distance on us. I think they must have radioed for overhead aircraft because we have experienced occasional vibrations from depth charges—nothing remotely close enough to do any harm."

"They are guessing. The sub's captain must have told the air force they pinged a vessel at a distance, but it has since disappeared. The aircraft probably dropped the charges at various intervals in the hope they might get lucky," said Lowell.

"They can only guess we are in the vicinity. It's night-time out there at the moment so, they can't see us from the air," said the chief planesman.

"They'll never catch up to us. We're at maximum speed and the Taft is the fastest submarine in the world. It's possible they will call up some corvettes if they're sure we're here."

Lowell turned to the sonar supervisor. "Keep me informed. You know what we'll be busy with— there'll be no formal speeches or goodbyes. It will just happen. I will return to spend the last moments with you."

He looked at each one in turn and then left for the wardroom. Hunt arrived at the same time and the two men sat opposite each other at their usual corner table. "Is everything ready?" Lowell asked.

Hunt checked his watch. "They will enter the torpedo room in five, sir. The time has come.

*

The weapon's engineer looked at the faces of the men behind him. The three techs continued with their cleaning charade while the engineer positioned himself at the battery inspection plate.

The five meter-long Black Shark torpedo rested on its belly at the open end of the tube and its structure gleamed in the overhead light. He removed the plate on the top of the housing in order to gain access to the A1-Ago battery, which provided power to the torpedo's electric motor. This would expose the battery terminals on which he would clamp the dragon clips of the cables. He then moved to the cover plate beneath which the firing mechanism attached to the warhead was mounted and prepared to expose the timer and fuse. Black Shark torpedoes did not detonate on contact but were designed to explode beneath the

hull of a vessel and break its back. When he completed the circuit from the battery, the fuse would
ignite the explosives, tear a hole in the side of the
sub and send them all to the bottom of the sea. The
entire process would take about twenty minutes.

∞∞

26

O'Malley and Coulson.

The prison warden received O'Malley and Gabby with cordiality. He sent them to the inmate visitor's center where they would interview Robert Coulson. On his own behalf, Coulson agreed to the interview with one provision: that O'Malley put in a word with the authorities with regard to Coulson's cooperation. Coulson was due to be tried in Missouri, a state which still retained the death penalty, for the assassination of President Martin Lewis.

The chief warder ushered them into a room with ten cubicles. Each had a glass screen and an intercom. O'Malley couldn't help recall the time of his first meeting with Coulson. The assassin, incarcerated in an FBI cell after his arrest by police, refused to submit to a sweep of his memory by Dr. Wheeler's latest invention. The FBI gave the assassin little option on the matter but as it turned out Coulson relented and was brought to the Neuro

Institute, where Lucas Wheeler and his assistant, Samantha Pink, worked.

O'Malley recalled the process of the memory sweep in its operation and the scary journey he, as the investigator, undertook into Coulson's memory banks. The device operated on the principles of quantum mechanics and used an avatar of information-bearing particles to first dislodge the consciousness of O'Malley's right brain and then transport it into the brain of the assassin. It had been an experience which exhilarated him but not one he would ever want to endure again. While part of O'Malley's consciousness resided within the avatar, he gained the impression and observation of his own physical presence within Coulson's memory.

While the experiment progressed, O'Malley's boss, the then assistant director of the FBI, Don Hadley, intervened and ordered the sweep to be shut down. Samantha Pink refused but sent a message to the avatar, run by a computer program called Echo, to warn O'Malley's right brain consciousness of the perilous decision. O'Malley realized his mind might be damaged by the sudden shutdown and he responded by the withdrawal of his consciousness, which returned back to his brain while he sat at rest in the lab. He equated the entire experience to a rollercoaster ride.

Ever since the conclusion of the experiment the long-term effects of his mind's entanglement with someone else's, became evident in the flashbacks. The irony lay in the useful information used by O'Malley to save his own life and those of his team. Despite this bonus he wanted to eradicate the effects.

When Coulson walked through the door into the enclosure on the other side of the screen, O'Malley looked twice before he recognized the assassin. Coulson's face looked tired and haggard and he must have dropped thirty pounds in weight. He sat down opposite them and lifted the phone.

"We meet again, Special Agent. I believe you need my help with something?"

O'Malley straightened in his seat and clutched the phone. Gabby listened in on a second receiver which allowed her to hear the conversation but not speak.

"I want you to know that I still see you as an assassin and a murderer, Coulson. The fact I need some information from you does not in any way mean I condone what you did."

"Spare me the lecture, O'Malley. I know what I did and who I am. I take responsibility for it and will no doubt pay the price for my actions. I don't regret assassinating Lewis—but I do regret the murder of the two innocent girls. If I could change that I wouldn't hesitate. Now—what can I do for you?"

O'Malley explained the flashbacks. "I saw you point to a trapdoor in the floor of a building, a small computer service business in Queens."

Coulson looked at him with astonishment. "I understand our minds became entangled through the memory sweep which you and that hippy professor performed on me—my guess is you saw an experience which involved me in my first two weeks of investigation with the secret service."

"You visited the business in question?"

"We did. I won't go into too much detail but it was a routine investigation of a certain Dr. Merlin Jones, who apparently made threats against a judge. When we arrived at the premises we looked around and found nothing of any real interest. I decided to look a bit deeper—that's when I spotted the trapdoor. It lead to a basement storage facility in which Jones kept a lot of cryogenic equipment."

O'Malley nodded. "Did you feel anything weird yesterday?"

Coulson considered the question. "Yes, in fact I did. I almost blacked out for no apparent reason while on my hour's exercise time."

"That explains this entanglement a little more but it's still a mystery what sparks it off. In the time of our need that trapdoor and storage room, saved our lives."

"Interesting," said Coulson. "But I'm sure you didn't come all this way to thank me, O'Malley."

O'Malley leaned forward and placed his elbows on the ledge below the screen. "You're right, Coulson. There is something else I see you doing, in what has been the focus of all the other flashbacks apart from the trapdoor episode."

"I'm listening," said Coulson.

"You mouth a word and I can't quite decipher what it is. I don't lip-read that well but it looks like 'power' or 'flower.' There is something you must know which might help us catch up with Jones."

Again, Coulson narrowed his eyelids. "I think I know what you might be referring to. While we were searching the premises I came across a file with the name 'Flower Information Technologies' written in pencil. It didn't mean anything to me, or the others at the time, so we left it."

O'Malley raised his eyebrows. "So, it was 'flower.' I think this might just help us find his present lair."

Coulson smiled. "I hope this will be enough material for you to catch him with. The grapevine has it that he is causing the government a bit of a headache."

"You have no idea just how much of a headache," said O'Malley.

"You will put in a word for me?" Coulson asked.

"I'll see what I can do but I make no promises".

Coulson nodded and stood. "I really regret the deaths of Gracie Beauchamp and her sister. I wish I could have those moments again—it would change a lot of things."

"I hear you, but it doesn't help those poor girls."

"Goodbye, Special Agent."

O'Malley nodded and replaced his phone. The warden peeked in from the door of Coulson's enclosure and saw that the interview was at an end. He came in, handcuffed the assassin and led him out of the room.

Gabby saw O'Malley wilt back into the chair and close his eyes. She knew he would relive the murders of the two girls. He always became silent whenever the subject came up and she perceived his mind returned to the loss of his own daughter.

"Let's get out of here, Dillon. This place gives me the creeps."

He didn't move but continued to sit in his chair with his eyes closed.

"Oh, honey. Don't go there—not now," she said. When he still didn't stir she wrapped her arms around him as tears of grief flowed down his cheeks.

*

An hour later O'Malley and Gabby sat in a coffee shop in D.C., each with a latte in hand. They drank in silence and cast each other an occasional glance until O'Malley broke the silence.

"I apologize for the little scene at the prison after Coulson left."

Gabby gave him a sympathetic look. "I understand, Dillon. Perhaps it's about time you moved on—it's been several years now since Fallon died."

"It just gets me whenever I have to discuss the two Beauchamp girls. I feel bad enough having to deal with that monster Coulson."

"He seemed genuinely saddened at having murdered them. I've read the reports and it appears he suffered a PTSD from the war in Afghanistan. He must have panicked when he realized they knew about his being blackmailed into the assassination."

"Let's not talk about him. I would rather talk about us," said O'Malley.

"Now, that's a subject I would like more clarity on," said Gabby.

O'Malley eyed her over the rim of his coffee cup. "I'm in a difficult place, Gabs."

She reached out and placed her hand over his. "Am I complicating your life, Dillon?"

"My life was complicated long before we met. Janet and I have never gotten over Fallon's death. I've always perceived that she blames me for being too liberal in my dealings with our daughter."

"I know the two of you have been to counseling—has any of it helped?" Gabby asked.

"Nothing has helped. I realize more than ever, that Janet and I are our own worst enemies. My marriage is not going to last, despite the fact you have come on the scene."

Gabby squeezed his hand. "Am I on the scene, Dillon?"

He smiled at her. "You are very much on the scene, Gabs. I realized how much I loved you when I thought you were lost to me."

"How will this complicate our working relationship?"

"I honestly don't know. I think we should keep it low profile for the moment, until I can sort things out with Janet. I have my son, Steven to think about as well and he will be the one in the middle, O'Malley answered."

"And then what?"

"There is no rule to prevent us from working together on the same team. It will be up to the director, though. Let's leave that for the future to take care of. I want you to know I intend asking Janet for a divorce. We can decide our future after that."

She looked down at their clasped hands. "I will not interfere, Dillon. I want you to know that I love you and care for you and I will wait for as long as it takes."

He leaned over the small table and kissed her on the lips. She closed her eyes and basked in the light of his attention. There remained a job to do and they both knew neither could afford to relax the effort to find Jones' lair. All else would have to wait.

They returned to the J. Edgar Hoover building to join up with MacDonald and Martinez in the briefing room. O'Malley shared his thoughts on the prison visit.

"I was right about the flashbacks. My mind and Coulson's are definitely entwined in a quantum entanglement of sorts. Whenever I am under stress and need an answer my right brain consciousness hooks up with Coulson's mind to look for answers."

O'Malley shared the details of Coulson's early secret service detail and their follow up on Merlin Jones.

Martinez asked the important question. "Was he able to help you with the mouthed word?"

O'Malley nodded. "He said they found a file with the name of 'Flower Information Technologies' written on it. I think this must have been some low profile business Jones had been using to further his ends,"

"So, we need to check up on this name?" Martinez asked.

"We need to find out everything about it. I believe we are getting close to finding Jones and his malevolent computer."

After O'Malley's request for another meeting in two hours, They all left the briefing room to see to personal needs "Nobody gets any sleep until we solve this thing."

Two hours later they gathered again in the briefing room. O'Malley shared some news.

"I have found something on Flower Information Technologies."

∞∞

27

Dr. Jones and Merlin's Lair.

MacDonald, Martinez and Gabby waited for O'Malley to elucidate on his statement.

"I've been doing a little research. Flower Information Technologies is an offshoot of Merlin Enterprises and is a company which Dr. Jones supposedly sold to another IT entrepreneur after his expulsion from the elite scientific community, for plagiarism. It is registered as an LLC, a small firm which fixes computer software problems based out of a private residence. The new owner is registered with the IRS but has shown no profit for the last five years. The director of the LLC is a person called Dudley Gomez."

"That name is familiar to me," said Martinez. "I can't put my finger on it but it will come to me."

O'Malley continued. "I searched the internet for a clue as to who Flower Information Technologies does business with and I found it on a website, set up by Dudley Gomez. It turns out Flower Information Technologies is registered as a subcontractor to do work for the FBI."

O'Malley's three team members all reacted to his statement. MacDonald jumped out of his seat, placed a hand on the back of his head and turned in a circle on his feet. Gabby's eyebrows arched like two rainbows and Martinez's mouth hung open like a cavern. For a few seconds they stared at O'Malley, dumbstruck by his words.

MacDonald spoke first. "You think this person may be working for Jones?"

"I think it's possible this Dudley Gomez might actually be Jones," said O'Malley. "Remember his plastic surgery—no one knows what he looks like."

Gabby posed the question. "Oh, for Christ's sake, Dillon. He works for the FBI?"

O'Malley narrowed his eyes. "He has a special clearance for work on the bureau's computers. Now I know why I knew the sound of the voice, just before Jones tried to blow us all to kingdom come."

"Oh my God. He has been right under our noses all this time." said Gabby.

"It explains how he accessed my computer," said O'Malley. He just recently sat with me though the installation of a new program he installed for all our agents. I kind of remember him now—a skinny guy with spectacles and dark-brown hair."

"Have you tried to locate him, boss?" MacDonald asked.

"He is not in the building at this time. I sent one of our police members to check on his business address and it's false," said O'Malley.

"Maybe he knows we escaped the blast and is onto the fact we know who he is. We're no better off," said MacDonald.

"Not exactly, Roland. I doubt whether he would know we've solved his identity charade. Did you check what shift he's on, boss?" asked Martinez.

O'Malley sat down at the computer and keyed in some instructions. A few seconds later he perused the shift roster for all the subcontractors, who did work for the FBI.

"He is due to fix some problems in the basement and on the second and third floors today—starts at 7:00 a.m. It's three thirty a.m. now, so we'll wait to see if he does come in. Here's a good photo of him, too."

O'Malley pulled up the employment file. The others crowded around the computer to look at the mug shot of the man who carried the name of Dudley Gomez.

"The sneaky bastard," said MacDonald.

"If he does come on shift what do you want do, boss," asked Martinez.

"We need to observe him and see what he does. If we confront him he'll just clam up. We need to find out where he is operating from, so that Merlin can be shut down. We have four hours; let's all get some shut eye." said O'Malley.

*

At 6:15 a.m. O'Malley and his team sat together in the briefing room with their eyes glued to the computer screen. O'Malley switched to the camera at the main entrance where everyone passed through security. The FBI personnel trooped beneath the camera, situated high above the double-glassed entrance doors. Some of the dayshift people started as early as 6:20 a.m. and the team waited in expectancy to see the man responsible for all the country's troubles.

"Keep it in mind that this person is intelligent and whatever happens we cannot allow him to escape our surveillance at any time. I have checked his routine for the day—he will be working on the internet receiving equipment in the basement.

Bear in mind that if Merlin is not stopped, millions of people will die."

"I find it strange he bothers with such a low-profile job. He could be safely working in some expensive lab or office and simply wait for the outcome of Merlin's work," said MacDonald.

"I think he enjoys interacting with people and let's face it—he chose the perfect place to keep an eye on things," said O'Malley.

The local FBI workforce started to pour in through the entrance and they craned their necks to make sure they did not miss their quarry.

"I spot him," said Martinez. "The guy with the dark blue windbreaker."

They stared at the image on the screen as Gomez looked up at the camera in the brief moment of his entrance to the building. Did he know they were onto him, or was it a self-conscious action of guilt? O'Malley considered the possibility Jones knew they were onto him. He experienced a tingle on his spine. Gabby must have felt the same because in the moment Jones' eyes unknowingly met those of his pursuers, she felt a sensation of fear. She reached out her hand and placed it on O'Malley's thigh. They glanced at each other and a sensation of trepidation ruffled the peacefulness of the briefing room.

"We need to get into position. If you come anywhere close to him and he looks at you please, for God's sake, don't show recognition. Gabby, you will be up here in the briefing room monitoring the floor cameras. We have our ear buds, so keep us informed of his movements."

She nodded. MacDonald and Martinez left for their designated floors and O'Malley waited until they rounded the corner in the passageway before he took Gabby in his arms and kissed her.

"I'll be back," he said.

She grabbed his jacket as he turned and pulled him toward her again. Her kiss conveyed the hunger she felt for his touch.

"Be careful. Jones is a ruthless man," she said.

O'Malley slipped into his own office to pull on a work coverall and pick up a small toolbox, prepared for the occasion.

Harry's Electrical Services displayed in large letters on the back of the coverall, in cursive writing. He removed a false mustache from his drawer and stuck it over his upper lip. A pair of spectacles with clear glass lenses came next before a final look into the mirror, which hung on the back of his office door. His own mother would not have recognized him.

O'Malley took the elevator straight down to the basement and disembarked. A few people walked to and fro, but in general not many of the FBI staff ever came down there. All the electrical panels and switchgear nestled in small alcoves and rooms off the main passageway, which led to the subcontractor's lunchroom. The J. Edgar Hoover building contained a lot of unused space and in the basement, five rooms of different sizes were rented out to the various contractors who worked there on a regular basis.

Each storage room door registered the name of a company. O'Malley, in an unconscious act, read them off in his head as he passed by. One of the names caught his attention. He stopped in his tracks after a few steps beyond the particular door as it registered in his brain—Flower Information Technologies, LLC. A sudden epiphany followed. Could this be where Jones kept some of his stuff? —might Merlin be situated in the room beyond the door?

"My God, right under our noses all this time. Is it possible?" O'Malley murmured. He turned back toward the door and tried the handle—locked.

"So, I guessed correctly, Special Agent."

O'Malley swung around to see the person of Jones, alias Dudley Gomez, behind him. "You knew we were onto you, Jones—didn't you?"

"I knew you would put two and two together eventually. I deemed it good timing as Merlin is about to complete our mission. The USS Taft is arriving in its final position and shortly the fireworks will begin. By the way, your disguise didn't fool me. I've been in your office—looked through your drawers."

The gun in Jones' hand indicated little chance for O'Malley to gain the upper hand, physically. His Glock lay in the toolbox. There would be no time for him to open the lid, extract it and shoot Jones.

"What do you intend to do with me, Jones?"

"My full title is Dr. Jones, Special Agent. While I'm holding the gun you can at least pay me some respect."

"How can I have respect for a man who is about to kill millions of fellow Americans because a

SWAT team accidentally killed his family and the government wouldn't recompense him for his loss?"

"You say it all too glibly, O'Malley. You surprise me for your lack of compassion. I know you've been through your own pain and understand what it's like to lose someone you love dearly."

"My loss is certainly a great one, Jones, but you don't see me taking it out on the citizens of the country."

"Perhaps you never really possessed the means, or the balls, O'Malley. I felt a sort of kinship with you because in some ways we are similar. We are both dedicated to our careers and we have both lost loved ones—to be honest, I was glad when you escaped all the traps Merlin set for you."

"Why would that be?"

"Because here you are and we meet face to face. You are the last surviving member of that ill-fated SWAT team, all of whom I vowed to kill."

"To extract an ill-fated revenge."

"I want you to understand, O'Malley—nothing matters after this. I am unfortunately a dying man. I have cancer of the pancreas and I don't have too much longer to live. Once Merlin has released the full payload of that sub, America will suffer over-whelming odds and within months, will fall to its enemies."

O'Malley, shocked into silence by his words, didn't know what to say. Jones threw a key to him which he caught with his free hand. "Open up. I want to introduce you to Merlin."

O'Malley shot him a dark look but complied. He moved into the semi-dark room, lit only by the light from a monitor and a row of green LED lights on a sophisticated computer, in the center of the room. Another panel of small LED's lit up and a digital voice spoke as he approached the table, on which the computer rested.

"Special Agent O'Malley—how good of you to visit our lair."

"You and your criminal boss have been difficult to find, Merlin—but I knew it would only be a matter of time."

"It's my pleasure, Special Agent. Dr. Jones specializes in surprises and this is the final chapter, where we win and the U.S. government loses."

Jones closed the door behind him as he entered. "I thought you might want to meet Merlin before I introduce you to your destiny, O'Malley."

"What else have you got planned, Jones? You are about to decimate the country with thirty nuclear warheads. There can't, surely, be a need for any further revenge than that."

"Then allow us to surprise you, Special Agent," said Merlin. *This whole building is rigged to explode. If you thought the small building in Queens made a big bang, it will be nothing in comparison to J. Edgar Hoover."*

"I get it. You want to wreak final revenge on the FBI for killing Dr. Jones' family."

Jones laughed out loud. "You are a clever one, O'Malley. I will give you that, but you wrote your own death warrant by being a member of this pitiful organization."

"It won't bring your family back, Jones."

"No, it won't. I will be going to meet my family shortly—I will leave nothing undone before I go."

"You're crazy, Jones. You are nothing but a bitter man who plays with quantum toys."

Jones turned to face the computer. The gun remained trained on O'Malley.

"Is the Taft in position yet, Merlin?"

"I will be ready to release the payload in a few minutes, Dr. Jones."∞∞

28

Tying the final Knot

Chief Petty Officer Hunt stood outside the closed door, which lead into the torpedo room. He prayed Merlin would be distracted by the many craft that followed them and not pick up the maintenance crew's movements. He did not think a computer could be distracted but if it were possible, this would be the ideal occasion.

A subtle change to do with the sub's momentum registered in his mind. The Taft fell silent, the cessation of all movement evident to Hunt. The sub appeared to be stationary and it struck him—they must have reached the optimum position to fire the missiles. The Taft's angle changed and they started a slow rise toward the surface. The ballistic missiles would under normal military circumstances, be fired at periscope depth. Hunt wished he could see the engineer's progress. He waited for the signal, a tap on the door from inside the room, to let him know engineer would be ready, and he thought of Sandra. Not much time remained on the clock for them.

*

The engineer wiped perspiration from his eyes. The nose cone would not budge. He needed to keep his cool and placed all his strength into prying it away from the five meter, long body of the torpedo. He glanced at his watch and spoke softly to himself. "Come on—you can do this."

The sub's forward momentum changed, a subtle vibration which experienced sailors picked up when a vessel slows and comes to a stop.

*

Commander Bill Lowell stood behind the sonar supervisor and watched the telltale enhancements on the console screens increase with a sudden intensity. The crew all knew the sub had come to a stop. The navigator's spot-on calculations, which pinpointed the optimum position to release the payload, featured as one small victory for them but brought a comfortless consolation to their world of hopeless options. The men stared with hollow eyes at the instruments and listened with detached impartiality to the acoustic signatures of the advancing armada and an anticipated quick end.

The Taft started its slow rise to the surface. On the way up, to the surprise of everyone, a strange occurrence took place.

*

O'Malley possessed no further words for his captor. He needed to overpower Jones before time ran out. The most important action would be to incapacitate the supercomputer before the explosive charges around the building could be activated. O'Malley needed to do enough damage in order to break the computer's contact with the sub. It appeared to be out of the question, however, but one possible solution still remained—the activated mic on his wristwatch. The others would be able hear the conversations between him and his captor. Gabby would have seen Jones take him a prisoner.

If he tried to extract the Glock from the toolbox he risked being shot on the spot. Jones appeared focused and ready to cut him down, should he try to go for his gun.

Merlin's digital voice filled the room and the row of LED's blinked on and off, in unison to the words.

"The Taft has reached the optimum position, Dr. Jones. I am initiating a slow rise to periscope depth."

Jones' evil grin stretched the lines on his face to the maximum. "In a few minutes the world will hear that America is no longer the great country it used to be. They will know that Merlin Jones took on the most powerful nation in the world and won."

"It's a shallow victory for you, Jones. All you will have succeeded in is the murder of millions of innocents."

"The U.S. government has those innocent's blood on its hands, O'Malley. Spare me the moral lecture—nothing will change."

O'Malley became conscious of a whisper in his ear. "We're outside the door, Dillon." Gabby's voice sounded gentle but full of purpose through the ear bud.

He couldn't answer back but strained to listen.

"You must try to distract Jones in some way. We are going to blow the door, so be warned—I hope you are not standing near it. Try to maneuver so that Jones is in front of the door. You have five seconds."

O'Malley knew what to do. He counted off three seconds, then threw the toolbox onto the floor. It landed close to Jones' right foot and the action caused the scientist to step to his left, a position which brought him in line with the room's locked door.

"What do you think you are doing, O'Malley?" shouted Jones.

The words were the last Jones ever uttered. The timing appeared to be perfect. The metal door of the room blew inward and caught him square on his back, with enough force to kill him outright. The blast threw O'Malley against the side wall of the room. A huge chunk of metal caught his head and he blacked out.

MacDonald's greatest fear stemmed from the action Merlin might take in the heat of the moment. They heard Merlin tell O'Malley about the explosive charges and they knew the AI might set these off. The plan to rescue their boss contained one possible flaw—the time elapsed between entry and the destruction of the computer.

Both MacDonald and Martinez held automatic assault rifles in their hands. They needed to find Merlin's position in the room and fire on the AI before it could trigger the sub's ballistic missiles and demolish the J. Edgar Hoover building.

The moment they heard Merlin tell O'Malley of the plan to detonate explosives, a fire drill alarm for all the floors except the basement warned the FBI staff to leave and security started a comprehensive search for possible devices. The action provided no guarantee of any success. They understood no one would be able to beat the speed of computation by the quantum processor but it depended on the instructions Jones might have programmed into the AI. Given the time frame to act, the FBI's plan to blow the door amounted to the best option.

MacDonald, first to enter the room, took in the scenario with a trained eye. The smoke from the blast still hampered their sight but he saw a table with equipment and started to unload the assault rifle at it. Martinez, who entered behind him, also drew a bead on the table and pulled the trigger. In the fraction of a moment, the equipment on the table disintegrated as both men started to fire with impunity. Bits and pieces from the super computer flew in all directions and more smoke filled the already acrid air. A haze floated throughout the room and started to billow out into the corridor.

Gabby's voice sounded anxious as she burst into the room and started a frantic search for O'-Malley but the smoke and haze made it difficult for her to see. With a final burst of gunfire, MacDonald released the trigger and observed the result of their rampage. The table lay in ruins on the floor and provided no evidence of any of the equipment it once carried. The computer lay in a thousand pieces and liquid nitrogen started to turn into gas as it escaped the cryogenic process. Not one LED light blinked and the circuitry lay on the floor, twisted and burned. Merlin no longer existed.

Gabby found the inert body of O'Malley and turned it over. The forehead bled from a nasty wound where the chunk of metal caught him. The pale, ashen face exuded the imprint of death. She brushed his hair away from the wound and screamed, "Medics—quick, agent down."

A nurse and the resident doctor of the FBI clinic, rushed in to help. The doctor couldn't help tender his surprise. "First it was you, Gabby—now it's him. What on earth has O'Malley tried to pull this time?"

Gabby looked through tear-filled eyes. "He has just saved millions of people but right now, you wouldn't understand that."

The doctor inspected O'Malley's wound. "He'll live—he's just another cat with nine lives."

MacDonald breathed a sigh of relief. "I guess Jones never expected any problems—he obviously never programmed Merlin to blow the building without his direct instruction."

*

Bill Lowell couldn't believe it. The air in the in the sub felt pure and clean as he inhaled. He took several deep breathes and filled his lungs. The others in the control room looked around in amazement as they, too, experienced the sudden cleansed atmosphere. Did Merlin decide to let them off the hook?

The chief planesman raised a hand. "Sir, I suddenly have control back. The AI has relinquished its control of our systems. Everything is operating normally again."

The men started to shout with joy in their amazement.

Lowell rubbed his chin. "Is Merlin playing a joke on us? As I understand it, the AI was just about to release the payload."

The sonar operator brought a measure of sanity back to the moment.

"Sir, the men in the torpedo room—they must be stopped."

Lowell turned and raced down the stairs into the corridor which led to the forward torpedo room. Chief Petty Officer Hunt still stood at the closed door of the room in expectation the men inside would let him know their preparations were well under way.

"We have control again—can't you smell the sudden cleanliness in the air?" Lowell shouted.

"What?" Hunt exclaimed. His bewilderment showed.

"We have to stop your men from sabotaging the torpedo," Lowell shouted.

"We can't. They have locked the door from the inside."

"Bring me something metallic and reasonable heavy—we'll try Morse code."

Hunt ran back to the galley and grabbed a large metal serving spoon. The bewildered cook gaped after him as he raced back to the torpedo room.

"Try this," he said.

Lowell's scant use of Morse code through the years concerned him but the alphabet still stuck in his mind from his university days. He tapped with vigor on the outer door: "STOP" and "OPEN DOOR."

They waited for a minute but to no avail. Lowell tried again. He hoped someone within the room would remember their basic training. On the third attempt the torpedo room door cracked open and one of the men stood there, his eye glued to the opening as he peered out at them with suspicion.

"Stop the engineer," shouted Lowell. "We have control of the vessel again."

The man disappeared and a moment later the engineer peered out at them. "You want me to stop the process? I have just managed to get into the fuse location."

"It is no longer necessary to scuttle the boat. The AI has relinquished control of all systems."

The maintenance crew looked at each other in disbelief. "If you had come a minute or two later, it would have been too late," said the engineer.

Chief Petty Officer Hunt felt weak at the knees. Their lives had dangled on a thin thread of probability but at the last moment a reprieve of gargantuan proportions had overturned the expected verdict.

"There remains one more problem. There are a dozen hostile craft in hot pursuit of us," said Lowell.

He sprinted back to the control room while Hunt raced back to the sleeping quarters to let Sandra know what had happened.

On Lowell's arrival in the control center he shouted to the radio operator. "Try to contact any one of those craft following us. Tell them we are no longer a threat and we have regained control of the situation."

'Aye, aye, sir," said the operator.

Hunt appeared next to him. "Let's hope they believe us."

Lowell looked around the control room, enraptured. "It's hard to believe the AI relinquished control. Something must have happened."

"They may have found out where Jones was keeping it," answered Hunt.

Several of the men in the control room bowed their heads and offered up silent prayers of gratitude.

∞∞

29

Janet and Dillon O'Malley.

Janet O'Malley knocked on the door of the apartment. Eight years of accumulated memories flooded her mind. The door opened and O'Malley greeted her with a peck on the cheek. She stared at him for a moment and then flung herself at him, winding her arms around his neck.

"I've missed you so much," she said.

The greeting took O'Malley by surprise. Janet's sudden show of love rocked his firm resolve and made him reluctant to share his latest decision. Their lack of contact throughout the duration of adversity created in him a notion; she considered their marriage to be over. Her verbal onslaught over his relationship with Gabby while he lay in the hospital bed in Harrisburg reinforced the idea that she considered their marriage to be irreconcilable.

She clung to him as they stood in the entrance and shed tears of grief. He held her close and whispered in her ear.

"It's okay, baby—it's going to be alright."

After what seemed an eternity she leaned her head back and looked into his eyes. "I've disappointed you, haven't I?"

O'Malley cast his eyes downward and didn't answer her question. "Let's go into the sitting room and talk," he said.

She let go and he turned to lead her, conscious of the sudden uncertainty in his mind. He knew he loved Gabby, but Janet was his wife. Their nineteen-year marriage teetered on the brink and a final close to the relationship frightened him. They sat down on the settee together, but at armslength. O'Malley took her hand and looked into her sapphire eyes—eyes that always held his own, spellbound. This night, however, they reflected hurt and frustration.

"How's Steven?" O'Malley asked.

"He's good—with his grandmother. He says hello."

O'Malley smiled. "I miss him so much and I don't want him to think I have forgotten about him."

"He misses you too, Dillon."

"I want to share with you, what I've been through over the last few days. It has just been de-classified—within a day or two everyone will know the details, anyway," said O'Malley.

She acknowledged his preparedness to talk about his work with a terse nod of the head. He told her about the nuclear submarine's abduction and the revenge sought by Dr. Jones.

Janet straightened up. "I remember that guy. You were involved on the SWAT team the night his family was killed."

O'Malley continued. He told her what happened at Three Mile Island on the night she rushed to the hospital in Harrisburg and the incident at Metro Station. He also shared the details of the explosion in Queens, which almost killed him and his team.

"I couldn't give up until I found Merlin's lair. The lives of millions of people depended on it."

He shared how Jones met his end, and the AI's release of the nuclear sub after its destruction.

Janet listened patiently and sympathetically until O'Malley completed his explanation, before she asked the most important question on her mind.

"I understand there have been challenges in your life, Dillon, but what about her?"

O'Malley knew it would come. He steeled himself to bite the bullet, but the answer stuck in his throat.

"You have to admit we've grown apart over the last few years, ever since Fallon's death. I know you judge me for not being strict enough with her, but until that fateful night, our daughter never got into any real trouble. It has been hard for me to go on knowing you hold that opinion," said O'Malley.

"Are you in love with Gabriella?"

The bluntness of the question made him uncomfortable. He knew the answer would cause immeasurable hurt.

"I never meant this to happen, Jan..."

"So—it's true? You do love her."

O'Malley couldn't coerce himself to say, "yes." He couldn't understand his reluctance to tell her the truth. Perhaps he felt ashamed.

"Have you slept with her?"

Again he hung his head. "It's not what you think...."

Janet stood to her feet to display her anger. Tears streamed from her eyes and rolled down her cheeks, unchecked.

"It's not what I think? Jesus, Dillon—listen to yourself. I know our marriage teetered on the edge, but you have pushed it over the precipice."

A sudden flash of anger took hold of O'Malley. "You are the one who brought me to the edge by your constant insistence I get over Fallon's death. I am a man, Janet—I grieve differently to you. I don't know how you were able to overcome the issue and get on with your life as though nothing has happened."

She stopped and stared at him. "I have never gotten over it, Dillon. I never will, but I realized for Steven's sake, for our sakes, I needed to move on and grab whatever happiness I could. I miss her as much as you do and yes, you are right—I do think you could have been stricter with her, but I never stopped loving you."

Her words cut into his conscience like a hot knife and he felt overwhelmed with guilt. Janet turned and reached the hallway in a few strides. She burst through the entrance and slammed the door shut. O'Malley remained seated on the settee. He wanted, in his heart, to go after her, but he knew it would not help the situation.

For a long time he remained seated and indulged a post-mortem of the entire saga. He brought the many positive aspects of their marriage to mind and all the good times. He contemplated his affair with Gabby and knew the blame lay with him. Janet's reaction to his infidelity did not surprise him. She only wanted the best for her family.

Their relationship, however, faced huge problems. Since the death of his daughter, an ever-widening gap separated their once mutual considerations. These considerations no longer held them together as a couple. Co-existence now relied on each being involved with their own form of escapism, his work and her church-related activities. On several occasions Janet tried to get O'Malley to attend services and accept council by her pastor, but he refused to be sucked into what he called an inhibitive and limited ideology. The religious scene remained an enigma to him and provided no answers to his problems.

When O'Malley surfaced from his contemplation, the lateness of the hour convinced him to sleep on it and make no further decisions with regard to the rest of his life. The decisions made over the last few days seemed shaky and in need of more consideration.

*

Janet O'Malley arrived at her mother's home in a state of depression. While thankful for a neutral place to stay while she sorted her life out, it felt like a journey back in time. The only difference between the present status quo and her teenage years rested in the absence of her father and the presence of her son.

Her mother met her at the door. "How did your meeting with Dillon go, dear?"

"Not well, mum. Please don't ask me for details—I don't want to talk about it."

"Of course, love, but I'm here if you need me."

"Where's Steven?" Janet asked.

"He's in his room. Did Dillon ask after him?"

"He did and I need to reinforce the fact his father loves him and is thinking of him."

Janet knocked on Steven's bedroom door and entered. Her son sat on his bed with ear buds on and a look of detachment written on his face.

"I've just spoken with your father, love. He's still tied up with the case he's working on and says he will see you soon."

Steven shrugged and continued to listen to his music. Janet's anger flared.

"Please be respectful enough to remove the earphones when I talk to you," she shouted.

He removed the ear buds with slow deliberation. "I heard you the first time, mother. You don't have to shout."

She felt an instant guilt and placed her hands over her eyes. How would she break the news to him? What would her son do when he discovered the truth about his father's affair?

*

O'Malley caught the elevator to his floor and walked down the long corridor to his office. The corridor opened up into a large space which accommodated a contingent of agents, all busy in their own small cubicles, each with a phone and a computer. As he entered the communal area, they all stood and began a slow clap of hands.

For a brief second the gesture failed to make an impression on him and he looked over his shoulder to see if the applause belonged to someone else. The realization struck him a moment later: the accolade belonged to him. MacDonald and Martinez, with Gabby in tow, stepped into the center of the room and waited. Gabby held a gift-wrapped box in her hand and stepped forward to where he had stopped. She handed him the gift and kissed his cheek.

"This is for you, Dillon—it's from all of us here in the office," she said.

For a moment, O'Malley did not know what to say and he stood before them, embarrassed, before words came to him.

"It was all a team effort. Everyone deserves this as much as I—in particular, you three." He gestured to the three of them. "I could not have done it without you guys."

He unraveled the gift wrap and opened the box to pull out a magnificent, gold wrist watch.

"You guys are spoiling me rotten," he said.

MacDonald cleared his throat. "We just want to convey our gratitude to you for your leadership, boss."

"—and for putting up with Diego," Gabby added. She gave Martinez a light shove and everyone laughed.

Martinez grinned. "I'm grateful our team is still intact. We could have all been in our graves by now."

"The boss is waiting to see you," said MacDonald.

O'Malley thanked everyone for the sentiments and the gift. He shook the hands of MacDonald and Martinez, then gave Gabby a hug. The touch of her skin on his sent tingles down his spine.

"Better not keep the assistant director waiting," she said.

He released her, walked through to his own office to deposit his gift on the desk and then walked further down the corridor to Ingram's office. He knocked on the door and waited for a response.

"Come in, O'Malley. Sit down."

The boss seemed to be in a good mood. "Thank you, sir," said O'Malley. He took a seat and waited for his boss to finish up on the computer.

A moment later Ingram looked up and smiled. "Congratulations, Dillon. The President of the United States is going to bestow an award on you. The ceremony will take place next week on Wednesday and will be held at the White House."

"The award should include my team, sir. I could not have achieved anything without them."

"They, too, will be honored but you will receive the award. It was your leadership which resulted in the defeat of Jones and Merlin. We are all infinitely grateful and I know it came at considerable cost to you."

"I was just doing my duty, sir. I did nothing anybody else couldn't have done under the same circumstances."

"Your humility is admirable, O'Malley, but the fact is you still did it. How's your head?" Ingram glanced at the dozen stitches in O'Malley's forehead.

"It's healing quickly. The stitches will come out in ten days and the doctor says the scar will not be that noticeable."

"Glad to hear it. After the ceremony I want you to take a little time off—spend some time with your family. I called Janet this morning and spoke to her at length. You really need to think about the consequences of your relationship with Gabriella. I know how hard it is to avoid close relationships in the work place. I feel a little responsible for being the one who assigns you your details. Gabby will be leaving your team—I have offered her a special agent's position."

O'Malley stared at Ingram. He felt like an animal caught in a trap.

"With all due respect, sir—is this necessary? Have you spoken to her about it?"

"Not yet, so please don't say anything until I have told her. I'm doing this to help you clear your head, O'Malley. We will see how promotion affects her decision to come between a man and his family. You have a teenage son you need to think about and I know this will not sit well with you, but the tribe has spoken."

O'Malley stood. He felt a flash of anger but did not want to cross the assistant director. "Thank you for your forethought and consideration, with regard to my domestic issues, sir. I will take the time off as offered. I need to process this. When will you talk to Gabby?"

"Right away," said the director.

O'Malley nodded and left the office. His thoughts bordered on panic and he felt a constriction in his chest.

∞∞

EPILOGUE

President Barrow stared out across the White House lawns and contemplated the possibilities of what might have been. His Chief of Staff, Eli Marion, sat on the settee with cup of coffee in his hand.

"We dodged a whole bunch of bullets, Eli. I don't want to think about what might have been if our guys didn't come through."

"I believe this O'Malley is quite the guy," said Marion.

"Not only will he receive the FBI Star award, but I believe the director will designate him next in line for assistant director," said Barrow.

"It will be a while before that happens, but I'm sure O'Malley will appreciate the gesture," said Marion.

"The USS Taft has put into the naval base at Nanoose, British Columbia and the crew are being flown to D.C. for the ceremony. They will receive medals for their part in staying alive throughout the ordeal. I believe they were on the point of sabotaging the sub when the AI released its hold on the system."

Marion took a sip on his coffee. "It was a close call."

"I got a call from the deputy Finance Minister. The major banks are to open for business today and the Internet is fully back online. People will get their lives together again."

Marion shifted in his seat. "When will you release the news about the failed coup?"

"I have called for a press conference tomorrow and all will be explained to the media," said the president. "There will still be fallout from the fact we hid the real dangers from the public, but I know we can weather the storm."

"You kept your head, Mr. President. Your administration will certainly see another term."

The president sat down behind his desk. "I never, for a moment believed otherwise, Eli. I think it calls for a celebration tonight, don't you?"

*

Commander Bill Lowell glanced around the room at his crew. The general staff at the U.S naval base in Nanoose, British Columbia extended their finest hospitality to the Taft sailors but Washington, D.C. awaited their collective charge and the crew looked forward to reconciliation with their families again.

"I want to thank all of you for your contribution to the security of our country. Our hearts are with the families of the brave men we lost and their remains will be flown by special military courier to John. F. Kennedy airport. You will all receive two weeks leave and on Wednesday, we will attend a special ceremony where the president will bestow a special award on each of you for valor. I am proud of you all. We overcame the most difficult odds, but I want to make mention of an FBI special agent whom we will get to meet at the ceremony. He will receive the FBI star. This is the guy who brought Merlin down and we all owe him a debt we can never repay."

The crew clapped and Chief Petty Officer Hunt indicated he would like to say a few words.

"Crew of the USS William Taft. I, too, am extremely proud to have served alongside you. I know we also want to thank Commander Lowell for his leadership throughout the events of the previous week. We are truly members of the most prodigious nation in the world and each one of you can be thankful there is a God above who cares about us."

The men all cheered and threw their caps into the air. It could have been a college graduation.

They all trooped out of the hall and prepared themselves for the flight to Vancouver, from where they would leave for New York.

*

O'Malley glanced at Gabby's face in an attempt to discern her thoughts.

"So, you spoke with Ingram?" O'Malley asked.

"Yes, I did. He wants to promote me to special agent and move me off the team."

"What did you say?"

Gabby gazed at the equestrian statue of Andrew Jackson as they sat side-by-side on a bench in Lafayette Park, a meeting arranged by O'Malley.

"I must admit it took me by surprise. I'm conflicted in that I don't want to leave you or the team, but equally, to make special agent is important for me. I really need to give it some thought."

"Did Ingram say where you would be posted should you agree?"

Gabby gave a half-hearted shrug. "He wants to send me to the US Embassy in Amman, Jordan."

O'Malley felt a pain deep in his heart. "Ingram must be crazy. So far from home?"

She nodded. "It would be difficult for our relationship, Dillon, if not impossible."

"What do you feel your options are?" he asked.

Gabby closed her eyes and leaned her head on his shoulder. "If I take the promotion I will effectively be placing our relationship on hold or even ending it. If I refuse, Ingram will most likely move me somewhere else and I'll still be out to sea. I might have to think of resigning altogether and finding other work. It's almost unthinkable."

O'Malley looked her in the eye. "Do you love me?"

"You know I do, Dillon, but the world appears to be conspiring against us. I feel a measure of guilt with regard to Janet and Steven. I'm really at a bit of a loss."

"I don't want to put any pressure on you, either, Gabs, but I can't resolve this issue for you. As painful as it might be, I will support any decision you make. May I suggest we wait until after Wednesday? After the ceremony is over, we will get back together and talk about it. In the mean time, we can check our priorities. I love you, Gabriella, and I don't want to lose what we have.

She lifted her head off his shoulder and offered her lips. He leaned down and kissed her with tenderness. In a few days, both would know their fate.

*

Wednesday arrived too quickly for O'Malley. He continued to wrestle with the future and oscillated between a new life with Gabby and the nineteen-year relationship with his family. A kaleidoscope of emotions raged in his heart and at times frightened him. The ceremony at the White House captured the festive mood of the people who attended it. O'Malley remained center attraction, alongside his team and the crew of the Taft.

The FBI Star, a beautiful medal of a small star in the center of a larger one, extended on the end of a white and purple ribbon, displayed like a military hero's pendant as it hung on O'Malley's chest. He felt truly honored to have the award bestowed on him, but uppermost in his mind remained the issue with Gabby's potential move. Would she choose him or her career?

After the ceremony closed, they left and walked down Pennsylvania Avenue together. The evening still young displayed a cloudless, star-studded heaven and O'Malley savored the warmth in the air.

Neither of them said a word until they came across a bus stop bench. O'Malley made a suggestion.

"Let's sit down here and take a moment to talk about the future."

She complied and they sat. He wrapped his arm around her shoulders and they were in silent contemplation for a moment.

"Have you come to any sort of a decision?" he asked.

She looked apprehensive and shrugged. "I have given it a whole lot of thought, but I am still conflicted."

"I, too, have given it my best, but before I share what's on my mind, I want you to know I love you very much and my suggestion comes at the expense of my own feelings."

She turned and looked at him, her features expressionless. "What are you saying, Dillon?"

He looked her straight in the eye. "I think you should take the promotion and see how it works out."

Gabby bowed her head and tears welled up in her eyes. She started to say something, but choked up.

O'Malley felt tears in his own eyes as he placed his hand on hers. "Sometimes we have to heed the ebb and flow of life, Gabs. I know it's hard—it's hard on both of us."

After a minute, the duration punctuated by an occasional sob from Gabby, she managed to talk again.

"I think you may be right, Dillon."

They discussed it for another half-hour and parted from each other with a deep sadness. He did not know how he would see out the rest of the evening, but decided to visit his favorite pub.

The bartender saw him enter and reached for a bottle of whiskey.

"The usual, Dillon?"

O'Malley sat and rested his elbows on the counter. "Thanks—double on the rocks, please."

"Had a bad day?" he asked.

O'Malley looked pensively at him. "Just another day at the office. Trying to keep my head on straight as usual."

The bartender laughed. "I know what you've been up to, mate, and thank God you did manage to keep your head on straight or none of us would be here tonight."

"You don't say," said O'Malley.

*

The next day O'Malley drove over to Baltimore and stopped in at his mother-in-law's home. She answered his knock on the door.

"Is she here?" O'Malley asked.

"She's here, wait in the lounge—I'll call her."

O'Malley sat on the couch. He didn't know what he should say and all he could muster when she walked into the room was, "Jan—please forgive me, I love you."

Janet closed her eyes and waited for her husband to come to her.

The End

More Books by Colin Setterfield

The Helium-3 Conspiracy

Love Sweat tears

Subduction Zone

*The A-Mortal Gene
*The habitat Relocation Project
*The Beautiful Planet
The Memory Hunter. Special Agent O'Malley
The Omega File. Special Agent O'Malley
Operation Terra Firma. Special Agent O'Malley